OWL OF THE DESERT

IDA SWEARINGEN

NEW VICTORIA PUBLISHERS
NORWICH, VERMONT

Published by New Victoria Publishers Inc., PO Box 27 Norwich, VT 05055
A Feminist Literary and Cultural Organization founded in 1976.

Cover Design Claudia McKay

Printed and bound in Canada
1 2 3 4   2006 2005 2004 2003

Library of Congress Cataloging-in-Publication Data

Swearingen, Ida, 1938-
  Owl of the desert : a mystery / by Ida Swearingen.
    p. cm.
  ISBN 1-892281-19-8
  1. Undercover operations--Fiction. 2. Young women--Fiction. 3. Ex-convicts--Fiction. 4. Revenge--Fiction. 5. Kansas--Fiction. I. Title.
  PS3619.W43O95 2003
      813'.6--dc21

                              2003008026

For Ellen. It would never have been possible without you.

Thanks are due to Melanie Livingston who knows makeovers and good coffee and to Gregg Peel, weapons expert and judge of fine beer. Also, to Barb Lakey and Marcie Rendon for encouragement, support, and the occasional kick in the butt. Thanks to the Corpus Christi Public Library for providing a wonderful space to work and to the Second Moon Coffee Shop where much of this work was written. I am also grateful to Ellen Hawley for her patience and endurance through many rewrites. Finally, many thanks to Rebecca Beguin and Beth Dingman at New Victoria Press for their editorial help and suggestions.

CHAPTER ONE

I am like a pelican of the wilderness: I am like an owl of the desert.
I watch and am as a sparrow alone upon the house top.

Psalm 102.6

Kate Porter spent twelve years planning her first day out of prison. First she'd go to one of those coffee places and find out what cappuccino really was. Then she'd go to a place with really great ribs where she'd have a cold beer and listen to the blues. What she hadn't planned on was sitting in the Lexington, Kentucky, bus depot enclosed by the dingy, mint green walls and watching kids with pierced eyebrows play video games while she waited for the three o'clock express to Kansas City.

She also wasn't prepared for how people would look out in the world. She'd seen so many photos of heroin-thin models and plastic television women that she'd come to believe people outside really looked like that. And here she was in the bus depot with a crowd of whey-faced, overweight people waiting for the dog to pull in so they could ride it to some godforsaken hole where they'd crawl off and eat chips and drink Cokes.

The sitting was getting to her. She glanced at her watch. It would be noon in Topeka, which meant it would be another hour before she could make her phone call. She picked up her second-hand Samsonite suitcase, threw her army surplus backpack over her shoulder and went outside.

She circled the block twice before coming to rest in front of a restaurant window. The smell of fried onions drifting out the door made her stomach tighten. She hadn't eaten since five A.M. but she couldn't get herself to go inside and order something. It looked like the place had a walk-up counter along with table service, and she couldn't figure out whether you sat down and waited for someone to bring you a menu or ordered at the counter. In jail, you had to know what you were doing every minute. Anytime you looked confused someone—a guard, another prisoner—swooped in and pulled you up short. She stood looking in the doorway until a man brushed past her to get inside, then she walked back to the bus depot and found a candy machine so old it had a mirror on the upper half. It gave her a glimpse of herself as she pulled the lever—oval face, tired eyes, a tightness around the mouth that surprised her. She could fill in the rest of the description with no help from the mirror. Her body was straight up and down—flatter than a board, her brother'd once told her. The arms were strong; years of working in the prison laundry did that. Glancing at her hands, she saw how red and sore they looked. The laundry did that, too. Looking back at the mirror, she tried relaxing her face, but the noise of the bus depot defeated her, so she contented herself with pushing her shaggy brown hair off her face. Her last bunkie had claimed to be able to cut hair. Like most of what she'd said, it had been a lie.

Kate pulled a Baby Ruth bar from the candy machine and settled herself in a salmon-colored plastic chair to open it. The chocolate was mottled with age, and when she broke the candy bar, it shattered in pieces, spewing peanuts on the floor. Prison made you neat. She bent and gathered each nut, hesitating between eating them and dumping them.

You're outside now, she reminded herself and dumped the nuts in an ashtray.

She ate the remaining pieces of the bar, chewing slowly. When she finished the last piece, she methodically rolled up the wrapper until it became a red and white ball, which she placed with precision in the chair next to her own. That would mark the space as hers and prevent anyone from sitting too close. She liked space—lots of it.

She passed an hour sitting there. Prison taught you how to do that. She kept her eyes on the bank of phones opposite her, waiting until a tiny woman with parchment skin and a brown wig completed her call. When she did, Kate stood up casually, no hurry, took her bags and made for the center phone. She dialed a number she'd called so often from the pay telephone just outside the visitors room at the Federal Women's Detention Center that she knew the charges for three minutes to Topeka, Kansas.

Dialing a strange phone reminded her of the former marine who had been her covert communications instructor at survivalist school. He stood, back straight, head shaved, lecturing at the top of his lungs.

"Use only public phones. Never use the same one twice in a row. Always make certain you are unobserved while dialing. Use your body to block the instrument keypad." He'd turned to demonstrate on a pay telephone he'd ripped off the wall of a convenience store when the owner refused to let him return a carton of spoiled milk. These days, he'd add instructions about the use of cellular phones—something Kate had only seen on television and heard about from other inmates.

The phone rang once, then again.

"Kansas Bureau of Investigation," a professionally cheerful voice answered.

Kate asked for Ray Gruber. When the voice asked who was calling she said, "Tell him its the Ornithologists Union."

The phone shifted to an interlude of tinny artificial music with a tempo intended to raise the listener's spirits. It only increased Kate's nervousness, and she paced at the end of the phone cord like a tethered animal.

"Hey, buddy." Gruber's voice had a forced cheerfulness.

"Seen any good birds lately?" Kate asked. That was the opening of the code sequence. Gruber would name three birds, the last of which would indicate where she could reach him.

"Hell, yes." His voice became expansive. She pictured him leaning back in his swivel chair, getting into the game. "Last weekend I caught me a great horned owl, a Kreider's redtailed hawk, and a whimbrel."

Kate made sounds of envy. "That Kreider's a hard bird to spot."

Gruber was into it now. He rattled on, giving her details about the bird's tail feathers and markings that would send any eavesdropper into a coma.

"Let's go out tomorrow, early," Kate said when he slowed down.

"Sure thing, buddy, but I gotta clear out my schedule. Call you back in about an hour, okay?"

"Right," Kate said, and replaced the receiver. Still standing by the phone, she stooped to search through her shoulder pack till she felt the slick cover of the *Field Guide to Eastern Birds.* She pulled it out and began thumbing through. Under the heading "Accidental Seabirds" was a handwritten list of bird names with numbers opposite. She ran her finger down the list until she came to whimbrel.

She slipped the book back into her bag and returned to the same seat in the line of linked chairs. Her movements were self-conscious, wary. She was coming from a place where every move telegraphed a message. Here, where no one paid any attention at all, she couldn't relax. A little boy ran past, a blur of blue overalls and yellow T-shirt. He caught an empty drink container with an arm and sent it crashing to the floor, then stood frozen for a moment, looking around, as if for a place to hide.

His mother, a worn-looking woman with lanky blonde hair, caught up to him, whirling him around to face her. "George L., you get back in that chair now before I push your face in." The boy fought her hold, struggling to squirm free, but the mother tightened her grip, turning her knuckles white. "Can you hear me?"

She pulled the boy in front of her and brought her face down until only inches separated them. Her voice grated like worn-out brake shoes. The child tried to match her glare, then, failing, burst into screams as his mother shouldered him like a bag of potatoes and marched off toward the restrooms.

An hour passed and Kate returned to the phones, this time dialing the number in her book.

The phone rang three times before Gruber answered. "I got you a room in the Westport Hotel," he said. "You're registered as Dana Lang. I'll be over tomorrow about eleven." He hung up without waiting for a response.

Gruber had first started coming around her old place at the

8

University of Kansas in the summer of 1982, during Kate's second year of college. From the first day of her freshman year, she'd gotten used to the idea of being followed around campus by bland-looking men in Plymouths and AMCs. Her father had taught her the rules when she was a child—never answer questions from strangers, never complete surveys, never talk to a government agent. He'd taught her to always assume she was being followed so she wasn't surprised when surveillance actually came. In fact, by the time it started she felt a kind of relief. Her father wasn't just being paranoid. THEY were out there—watching.

She had lived in three tiny rooms on the upper floor of a Victorian house that had been converted to a rabbit warren for students. An outside stairway connected her apartment to the backyard, and on a humid early morning in July she'd taken her coffee down to drink it in the yard. She was staring into her cup when she heard the ancient metal gate squeak behind her and looked up to see a tall, rumpled man walk through it. He was wearing wrinkled khakis topped with a white short-sleeved shirt that bulged over his belt. The heat had curled his dark blond hair into damp ringlets around his forehead, which must have blurred his vision because he brushed them back to look up into the oak tree in the middle of the yard.

He had stared up for a moment then turned to her. "White-breasted nuthatch." He pointed up to the tree.

Kate followed his hand until she saw a neatly patterned grey and white bird making its way headfirst down the trunk of the tree.

"Nice, huh?" the man said.

Kate nodded, watching him from the corner of her eye.

He smiled at her—a big smile, so big that she found herself involuntarily returning it and taking his extended hand.

"My name's Gruber, Ray Gruber, with the Kansas Bureau of Investigation." He reached for his identification, but Kate motioned to stop him.

"I won't talk to you," she said.

He nodded and took a step back. "You wouldn't have any more of that coffee, would you? I had to leave early; I sure could use some right now."

Kate knew it was a ploy and started to refuse, but something stopped her. It was early, the beginning of another heat-soaked day, and the overgrown yard already shimmered with humidity. It was only a cup of coffee—she wouldn't let him in the house.

Gruber waited beside the lower steps while she went upstairs.

"Sugar?" she called down.

Gruber was creeping around the tree as if he were stalking something.

"Just cream," he yelled.

When she brought the coffee down, they sat side by side on the bottom step, drinking in silence. Then Gruber stood up and slowly circled the tree.

"There's a pair of titmice in there, too." He moved his head to motion upward. "Do any birdwatching?"

Kate shook her head.

"Got into it when I was a kid," Gruber said. "Its just like hunting except you don't bring anything home."

He must have made that joke a thousand times but Kate laughed anyway.

"I need to talk to you about the American Patriotic Front."

He turned to face her.

Kate looked into the distance, studying the decaying door of the garage at the back of the lot.

"They say the APF's behind some bank robberies. Word has it your dad's the man planning them." He sipped his coffee and continued looking at the tree. "You probably don't know it, but the KBI was founded to catch bank robbers. We chased after some big ones— Pretty Boy Floyd, Ma Barker, even the Barrow Gang."

Kate looked over at him. For a second she wondered if he saw her as Bonnie Parker or Ma Barker.

"I know they're not just robbers—they think they're doing it for a cause, but this keeps on, someone's going to get killed."

Kate looked away uneasily. She'd said almost the same thing to her father the last time they talked. He'd told her about the sacrifices he and his men were ready to make. Kate hadn't argued, but a question still haunted her—What about the bystanders?

Gruber set his cup down on the peeling wooden step. He pulled a wallet from his hip pocket, extracted a business card from it and, balancing the card on the stair rail, wrote a number under a line of print.

"Here's my home number. You give me a call if you ever want to talk."

It was almost two years to the day before she called him. By that time, Gruber's prediction had come true—someone had been killed. It was at a bank robbery in Hutchinson, Kansas. The vice-president's secretary had taken a stray shot and died in Kate's arms. Kate had been on the run for two years, but on that hot night in Champaign, Illinois, she'd decided she it was time to stop. When he answered the phone, Gruber's voice was thick with sleep.

"Seen any good birds lately?" Kate asked and began her second life.

CHAPTER TWO

The lobby of the Westport Hotel looked as if it had once been carpeted and filled with grand ferns and tropical plants with unpronounceable names, but like the Lexington bus station it had been seized and occupied by rows of salmon-colored plastic chairs molded to fit the contours of an unknown species. Someone had worried about stickups enough to add a Plexiglas cage to the original marble of the registration desk, and right now it protected a pear-shaped man whose T-shirt barely covered the layers of fat on his stomach. As Kate approached he looked up, squinting as if she were difficult to see.

"A reservation for Dana Lang," Kate said.

Without looking for her name, the clerk handed her a key.

"That'll be fifty dollars."

She started to ask for the elevator, but the clerk, as if to ward off the possibility of conversation, nodded toward the back of the lobby.

Kate didn't care that the hotel room was almost as bare and drab as the dayroom at Lexington. She dropped her bags, fell onto the bed and slept in her shirt and underwear, too tired to shower or unpack. When she woke she lay still, listening to the muffled footsteps in the hallway. She smiled, savoring the quiet. Days at Lexington had been a din of shouts, boom boxes, and garbled metallic voices making announcements over the public address system. For her first four years she'd shared a cell with a woman who talked to herself all day and made glottal, wet sounds all night. Her second bunkie couldn't imagine talking at less than a shout. And then there were the women who woke in the night screaming with terrors too deep to penetrate the light of day. Kate stretched, extending her toes toward the far corners of the bed. Quiet, solitude, and space. It was beautiful.

Finally, she rose to take her first shower as a free woman, using all the hot water she wanted, drying herself slowly. Even the thread-bare towels felt fresh and soft. Showers at Lexington had been a dangerous business. Male guards lounged in the doorway, smiling as if they were at a strip bar. And then there was the chance that you'd pissed off some gangbanger from Chicago, and she was waiting in the steam to jump you.

Downstairs, she roused the clerk from his stupor and tipped him five dollars to give Gruber a note when he came. Then she set out on foot for a collection of shops called The Plaza.

She remembered this part of town from her college days. She walked slowly, stopping to examine the window display at a hardware store, then a carpet outlet. A carpet sample, a new kind of wrench—it was all as involving as looking at the Hope Diamond. When she eventually moved on, she saw three black teenage girls practicing dance moves and laughing while they waited for a bus. Farther down she passed houses with piles of dry leaves waiting to be bagged and fought the urge to jump in the middle and cover herself with them.

The cafe was just where she remembered it, facing a fountain with water spouting out of lions' heads and dolphins. Inside she was shown to a booth and left to leaf through an oversized menu filled with glossy photos of food and elaborate descriptions that made each dish sound as if it were the one thing guaranteed to bring absolute happiness.

"What'll it be dear?"

To Kate's relief the waitress was of the old school, wearing no-nonsense shoes and a fluffy handkerchief pinned to the chest of her uniform.

"Two eggs, sausage, and toast."

"How'd you like those eggs?"

Kate paused, unprepared for the question. She frowned a moment. The waitress stood over her, order book ready, waiting.

"Over easy?" Kate raised her voice as if she were asking permission. The waitress made a note of her choice.

"Coffee?"

Kate nodded.

She was still eating when Gruber shuffled in the door and stopped to scan the room for her. His hairline had receded, the blond ringlets were streaked with grey, and his midsection had grown heavier, giving him a gut that hung over his belt and made it even more difficult for him to keep a shirt tucked in. But the grin he flashed when he saw her was just the same, although when he came close she could see more lines around his eyes and the beginning of a double chin.

Kate stood up to greet him. For a second they both hesitated, Kate starting to extend her hand, Gruber opening his arms, until they moved together to hug.

"You look good," Gruber said, as if surprised.

Kate shrugged.

"Jailhouse muscles." She smiled, "Looks like you been living good, too."

"Too good," Gruber patted his midsection, "but I'm working on it."

Gruber had gone with her when she surrendered to the federal marshals, and he'd gotten her a lawyer, even when she said she didn't want one. All she wanted to do was plead guilty and go to jail for the rest of her life. But Gruber had gotten her a deal—testify before a federal grand jury and do twelve years.

She'd taken the offer and recited every detail she'd ever known about the American Patriotic Front. She'd named names, described meeting places, recited the proceedings of secret meetings to the best of her recollection. Her father, Bud Porter, was still at large, and the FBI wanted him a lot.

Gruber had stayed off to one side during her interrogation and testimony. Sometimes he brought her cups of coffee and sandwiches so she wouldn't have to eat jailhouse meals. They didn't talk much, and when they did it was about birds. Her time in hiding had been lonely, and she hadn't slept well, so she'd started taking long walks at dawn peering into trees, trying to pick out which of the half-dozen songs she heard came from the birds she actually saw. They talked about schools—he'd gone to Washburn University in Topeka—and football. She didn't give a damn about the game, but Gruber didn't let that stop him from going on and on about the NFL.

14

He'd showed her pictures of his wife, who loved dancing, and his daughters, who didn't. He talked about playing high school football in Pittsburg, Kansas, and his hero, Alvin Dewey, the Kansas Bureau of Investigation agent who tracked down the killers Truman Capote wrote about in his book *In Cold Blood.*

They stayed in touch after she got to Lexington. Gruber was the one who kept it going, writing or calling to tell her about his progress, or lack of progress, in tracking her father and occasionally asking her opinion of leads. She expected him to move on to other things but time passed, and he didn't forget about Bud.

In their letters, they'd talked about loneliness, the migration patterns of sandhill cranes, one-night stands, and the sorry state of American League baseball. Gruber had written about his divorce and how much he missed his two daughters. In the middle of a letter explaining how to prepare liver and onions on a Bunsen burner, Kate had broken down and written the whole sob story about her failed affair with another inmate and the auditory hallucinations that left her sitting in a corner wailing like a baby after a two-week stay in administrative segregation.

It had been Gruber's idea to use a code based on bird names in Roger Tory Peterson's *A Field Guide to Eastern Birds.* Kate told him it was dumb, but he claimed he'd always wanted to have a club with a secret code.

Gruber maneuvered himself into the booth opposite her, cleared his throat, then slid a heavy manila envelope across the table.

"You been keeping up with things?" he asked.

Kate shook her head.

"This is what I've got from the last six months. My take is, your father's going to surface down in Texas. If I'm right, we could head down there and snatch him up." He paused and unfolded a paper napkin. "We got a call from a detective in the San Antonio P.D. with a lead. Woman told him about going over to her boyfriend's house. She says he was with the American Patriotic Front and there was an old man staying there. The boyfriend got real nervous that she saw the old guy."

"Is she a snitch?"

Kate knew from experience that snitch information was imaginative, embroidered, and often false.

Gruber shrugged.

"Anybody get her to I.D. him?"

Gruber shook his head.

"I'm flying down there Tuesday," he said.

"He still there?"

"She hasn't seen him again. She thinks her boyfriend might have moved him out."

The waitress returned to take Gruber's order.

"Two pieces of toast, no butter, small OJ, and coffee."

The waitress looked down at him disapprovingly.

"Got cholesterol problems."

Kate nodded and pushed the remains of her sausage under an uneaten piece of toast.

"Oh," Gruber called after the waitress. "Could I have skim milk with that coffee?" He waited until she was gone. "You still think you ought to try and draw the old man's attention?"

"I think I've got the way to do it."

They'd argued over and over about the best way to catch her father. Kate had started out wanting to find him and kill him. Short and simple. But Gruber gradually convinced her that it was better to set a trap for him and take him alive. She had to admit that her father doing fifty years in a maximum-security hole with twenty-four-hour lockup was good. He'd never see another human being except the guards who shoved his food through a hole in the door. Jailhouse Aryans would make him a hero, and some of the guards might agree. There was no way to stop that from happening. But any way you looked at it, twenty-four-hour lockdown was jail time as hard as it got.

"You remember I wrote you about that money my grandma left me?"

Gruber nodded.

"Well its been sitting in the Tascosa State Bank in Amarillo for the past six years, waiting for me to get down there and claim it. I'll go to Amarillo, get my money. My guess is Daddy's got somebody watching that account. It's the only way he could be sure to hear when I got out. The minute I touch it, it'll be like running a flag up a pole."

"If he knows you're in Amarillo, won't he have somebody take you out before you hit the city limits?"

Kate gave him a slow smile. "That's where the fun starts. I can run circles around those ol' boys down there. You just get down to San Antonio and see if you can pick up his trail."

Gruber still looked doubtful. "Maybe you ought to leave some of that money there till we get finished so you'll have something when this is all over." His voice trailed off, leaving a question hanging in the air.

Kate shook her head. That money was her last tie to a history she wanted to terminate. She couldn't be shed of it fast enough.

Gruber leaned back and ran his fingers through his hair, reflecting. Then he reached inside his jacket and extracted a second, letter-sized envelope. "Here's what you asked for."

He opened it with a shake, and some plastic cards fell out on the table. Kate examined them—a Kansas driver's license made out to Katherine Alice Porter, a social security card, a photocopy of her birth certificate, and a stack of twenty dollar bills secured with a rubber band.

"How much is in that bank account?" he asked.

"Ten thousand dollars last time I heard."

"Good. You owe me five hundred."

Gruber insisted on driving her back to the hotel. "You flying to Texas?" he asked.

Kate shook her head. "Bus."

When he looked surprised, she said, "I've got a stop to make along the way."

Gruber nodded like he understood, but she wondered. Once she'd asked him why this case mattered so much.

"Just once in my life, I want to land the big one," he told her.

Seated across from him now, she could picture him standing outside a courthouse while some classy blonde from New York interviewed him. He'd recite the details of his relentless search for a dangerous political fugitive, and he'd smile modestly into the camera. She searched the crowd for herself, but she was nowhere in sight.

CHAPTER THREE

Back in her room, Kate sat cross-legged in the middle of her double bed, spreading the material from Gruber's envelope into piles. There were articles about the early years of the American Patriotic Front, complete with pictures of her father, her brother and herself in combat fatigues. One was captioned, "Bud Porter and the next generation of American Patriots."

She'd forgotten how handsome her brother Dwight was in those days. He was always one step ahead of her—in school, in baseball, in the militia their father organized. In that terrible period after their mother's death, when their father withdrew from them for days at a time, they'd drawn together as close as twins. But later he was her rival. He was the sun; she'd never be more than the moon.

She grew into a wiry tomboy, a bookworm and a loner. Dwight inherited Bud's genial manner. Everywhere he went, he drew people to him. He practiced tough looks in the mirror when he thought no one was watching, and he made himself walk with the ramrod stiffness of a drill sergeant, but nothing could conceal his essential grace.

Among the clippings about the bank robberies, she found a report written by Gruber, tracing the pattern of robberies by the size of the bank and the economic conditions of the surrounding farms. He predicted that the First State Bank of Hutchinson, Kansas, was a prime target. Kate nodded as she read. It was a nice piece of work, and he'd been right on the money.

The next sheaf of papers was about the search for Bud Porter after he'd gone underground—reports from police and sheriffs' departments in Alaska, the Colorado Rockies, Idaho and Arkansas.

There was only one file from the feds, stamped confidential, about an incident where they'd gotten a tip that Bud was working at a cafe in New Mexico. The dry language couldn't hide the comedy of errors that followed. Bud must have spotted their stakeout, because he had pizza delivered to the agents and then vanished. He wasn't seen again for six months.

Gruber had also included some more recent articles, written after the Oklahoma City bombing. These were long pieces, tracing the rise of the militias. One, in the *Chicago Tribune*, called Bud the godfather of the militia movement. The writer quoted a passage from Bud's book, *Survival in a Time of Tyranny*, where he called federal agencies citadels of oppression and said they should be targeted for direct attack. Another article, this one in the *Kansas City Star*, described Bud as the puppetmaster of the far right, manipulating recruits like Timothy McVeigh into carrying out his master plan.

Kate shook her head in surprise. The way the papers talked, Bud Porter was the master criminal of the decade. It was a long way from the man she remembered seated at a dusty desk sifting through papers.

The last articles were about Dwight after the accident—his time at Baylor University and the founding of the Gospel News Network. There were photos taken on the set of his television program, at public events alongside Oral Roberts, and an old one with Jim and Tammy Bakker.

She remembered when he'd flown out to Wichita during her trial. He must have had pull with somebody because instead of meeting in the visitors' area, where you talked through bulletproof glass, they met over one of the metal tables reserved for inmates and their attorneys. The chaplain rushed in to shake Dwight's hand.

"It's a privilege to meet you, Brother Porter."

Kate wondered where they got the brother stuff. The chaplain nervously asked if Brother Porter wanted to take a moment for prayer.

"I think we would like a moment of silent communion together," Dwight said.

The chaplain looked flustered, but he gathered himself and backed out of the room.

Kate bent to Dwight's wheelchair to hug him. The cloth of his suit was a smooth wool. It felt expensive, and he smelled of an aftershave much gentler and rarer than the kind worn by the heavy-faced lawmen and agents she met with every day.

He brought gifts—a box of Snickers bars, two cartons of Camels, and twenty dollars in cash. And, probably because he was Brother Porter, he was also allowed to bring a box of fancy cookies with the label of a French bakery in Georgetown.

"How they treating you?"

"Okay."

Dwight nodded and looked uneasily at the motes of dust floating in the sunlight that streamed in between the bars of a high window.

"They say you're going to plead guilty."

Kate nodded.

He tried arguing her out of it, but Kate wouldn't give in.

"Well at least let me get you a decent lawyer. Hell, I can get that guy from Yale, who is he? Dershowitz? I'll get F. Lee Bailey out here for you. He'll knock the socks off these ole boys. Get you the best deal in town."

"Thanks, but I'm okay with what I got." All she wanted to do was enter her plea and start serving her time.

Dwight shook his head helplessly. For a long moment, neither said anything. Then he shifted in his chair. "Any word on Daddy?" Dwight said.

"Not a thing."

"Yeah," Dwight stared at the floor. "He's gone to ground. They'll never get him." He brought himself back. "Let me ask you something. Why'd you give yourself up, Katie? You could have done just what he's doing. You did for two years."

"I couldn't stand it anymore." She lowered her head. Even saying it was hard. "We killed that woman. I killed that woman."

"Katie." Dwight leaned forward and took her hand in his. "We both know who pulled that trigger and it wasn't you."

She started to say she knew that, but Dwight shook his head to silence her and kept on talking.

"The man responsible for your being here and for this—" he patted his legs—"is running free."

Kate looked at him, surprised. She'd never heard him talk this way before.

"I'm a cripple, and you're going to federal prison, while he's out there playing soldier and acting like a hero."

He looked off into the distance again. Kate saw his jaw twitching as he fought to control something—rage or pain probably, but she wasn't sure which.

"I promise you this. He'll pay. I will make sure of it. He will pay." Dwight said. He spoke slowly, like a man pronouncing a death sentence.

Once she was in Lexington, she phoned him from time to time.

"Katie, I have some friends. We could start working on parole." He said.

"I don't want parole."

"Well, at least let me get you moved to minimum security. Make it easier for you. It doesn't have to be this hard."

There was no way he could know how tempting that was. She was in a high security unit where the conditions were enough to draw Amnesty International's attention. Surveillance cameras all over the place, even in the shower; lockdowns; full body searches. You had to get special permission just to make a phone call. Then you stood in a line of women—always the lines of women, yelling and screaming at each other to hurry up. Life was nothing but Klaxon horns, midnight screams, and the constant sound of metal slamming into metal. At a minimum-security facility, she'd sleep in a room instead of a cell, shower anytime she wanted, maybe work in a garden instead of the laundry.

She shook her head as if he'd be able to see her. "Thanks anyway." He didn't understand, and she couldn't explain. The truth was that she needed to do hard time because she believed that every full body search, every slam of the cell doors, every daily indignity was a step toward atoning for Viola McKinnon's death. She held onto the hope that if she endured long enough, she'd stop seeing that woman die.

In time, she quit calling. They seemed to have less and less to say. Someone, probably his administrative assistant, continued sending packages though. Every couple of months she'd get two cartons of cigarettes and a money order for twenty dollars. For an hour or so she'd feel like the richest woman in the world. Cigarettes to trade, cash in her account.

Dwight's show had gone national by then, and some of the women in the dayroom watched it every day. Kate had a hard time believing that the unctuous man in tailored suits and heavy gold cufflinks was her brother. He interviewed celebrities, led healing prayers and read letters from the saved. Every ten seconds, messages flashed across the bottom of the screen urging viewers to send money immediately to save the ministry. The ministry always seemed to be in trouble; every show there were the same pleas and threats that the ministry would end without immediate financial support from every single viewer.

She was in the dayroom once with her friend Shabeeka when someone turned on his show.

"Shit, Shabeeka, that man must be raking it in." A woman who'd been convicted of setting fire to her three grandchildren sat in front of the TV set, watching as if it were a holy shrine. She gave Kate a sideways look. "You get out of here you ought to go let him save you."

"When pigs fly." Kate gave a bitter little laugh.

"That kind of money, he can save my whole family," Shabeeka said. She frowned in concentration then turned toward Kate again. "He don't believe that stuff, does he?"

Kate had shrugged. Who knew what Dwight believed?

Now, looking at the photos spread in front of her, Kate missed Dwight desperately. She always had. But there was no way she'd call him until this was over. There was no reason for him to be involved in this. What she had to do now, she would do alone.

She put the papers to one side and lay back on the bed. It was easier to think about her father. She'd spent years trying to figure out where he was hiding. From her own experience, she knew that staying out of sight was the easy part. What finally gets to most fugitives is the loneliness. Men make do with whores and crowded bars.

22

Women can bury themselves in relationships but sooner or later people start asking questions. In her time, she'd spent weeks without saying more than hello to anyone. The closest she'd gotten to a relationship was a stray cat that moved into her place in Denver, and she'd had to leave it behind when her boss asked questions about her Social Security number.

It might be different for Bud. He could be nested with any of the hundreds of militia groups that trained all over the country. He could be holed up in a cabin in Montana. He could even be living with skinheads on the West Coast.

She rolled over and saw a newspaper clipping from the *Wichita Beacon,* which showed her leaving Sedgewick County Courthouse sandwiched between two deputies, hands chained to her waist. She was looking at the ground with an expression so heavy it didn't look like she'd ever hold her head up again.

She rose from the bed and crossed to the bathroom mirror to examine herself. Her eyes were less haunted, but she still had the look of a woman who'd been used hard. Returning to the bed, she gathered Gruber's papers and stuffed them into her backpack.

CHAPTER FOUR

In the morning, she took a bus to Wichita, where she changed to another that would take her through the town of Greensburg. The trip was slow and bumpy, and she leaned hard against the window to escape the stale wine smell of the man sitting next to her. On the other side of the aisle, an exhausted-looking teenager with a baby sat in the midst of so many plastic bags that it looked as if they'd taken up residence. The child was fussy, and the mother rocked gently, trying to comfort him, but nothing she did kept him from wailing every time the bus hit a pothole. At first Kate leaned forward, watching the winter fields and faded barns pass by. Things hadn't changed much since the last time she made this trip. Finally she leaned back in her seat and closed her eyes.

She'd driven this road with her father and the boys on the way to rob the First State Bank of Hutchinson. She was a last-minute substitute pulled into the job to replace Wayne Griggs after he broke an ankle tripping over his daughter's Big Wheel. Kate had always thought of Griggs as a fuck-up. The only reason he was on the squad in the first place was that he'd been a school friend of Dwight's.

She was in her sophomore year at the University of Kansas. She'd been on her way to chemistry class when a man in a grey truck hailed her. She had to look twice before she recognized her father underneath the dark cap and scraggly beard. He'd been underground ever since the robberies started. Police in three states were looking for him, and here he was in the middle of campus.

She made herself walk to the truck. Bud motioned for her to get in.

"Daddy, I've got classes. I can't just leave." She looked around her hoping someone would come along and give her an excuse to take off.

"We need you, Sister." Bud gestured toward the passenger door, assuming she'd take her seat beside him. She hesitated—she could just turn away and leave him—then she made the mistake of looking him in the face. His butane blue eyes seemed like they were cutting a hole through her chest. Part of her wanted to say to him, Daddy, I can't go anywhere with you. I'm beat. I was up till two A.M. discussing the U.S. role in third world development. I was talking to a couple of my roommate's friends from Africa, and you know what? They're smart. They speak French and English and have better educations than I do. Oh, and I've got a coffee date right after class. It's with this girl from down the hall. I think I might be in love with her.

But there was another part of her, the good little soldier, that fell right into place. Colonel Bud Porter was not a man you said no to.

"God help us," she said softly.

Bud frowned. "You've changed."

Kate swallowed slowly. "I got my hair cut."

Bud nodded. "Just get in," he said. "We'll talk on the way."

And like a marionette on a string, she slid her backpack off her shoulder and got into the front seat. Her father put the truck in gear, and she looked out the window. She took a long look at the campus as they passed. Maybe he just wanted to talk, and she could still make that date with Jennifer.

On the way to Wichita, Bud outlined the plan. He'd be the driver. They'd pull a stolen van in front of the bank. The back would open, and the squad would rush the lobby in a burst of noise and motion— three heavily armed people dressed in battle uniforms topped off with black ski masks. She knew both the regulars, Delbert and Eddie. Delbert had done five years for armed robbery in the Texas State Penitentiary at Huntsville, and it had left him with a jagged scar down one side of his head and a set of jailhouse muscles. He'd handle the teller. Eddie was a nervous little guy with greasy dark hair. He'd go behind the counters and collect the cash.

Kate would herd any customers off to the corner where the bank president and his secretary had their desks. Once they had the cash, they'd fire three shots at the ceiling and get back to the van. Bud would drive across the prairie to an abandoned farmhouse people still called the Ditton place. They'd ditch the van and split up, taking the two pickups they'd stored there.

As she listened to her father talk, Kate felt herself nodding in agreement and saying, "Yes, sir." But she couldn't stop the questions that kept popping into her mind. Is violence the best way to achieve a political goal? Are crimes justifiable if they are done in the name of the cause? They were the kind of questions people argued about late at night over coffee and cigarettes—the kind of questions that would make her father think she had doubts about his goals. She didn't ask them. Instead, she emptied her mind the way good soldiers do before an operation.

"It'll be another victory for the American farmer," Bud said as they drove through the barren grey mounds of the Flint Hills. Kate knew the speech by heart. Banks represented the Jewish conspiracy to cripple independent American farmers and hand the country over to communists and lesser races. Only armed resistance could stop the conspiracy in its tracks. Kate looked uneasily out the window. A hawk was floating on an updraft, waiting for prey. Safe inside her father's truck, she felt its eye on her as if she were a field mouse crouching below.

Things went wrong from the start. Eddie's job was to steal the van. He picked a Ford Econoline parked outside a bar. It was clean and white—Eddie had a weakness for white. He opened the door and was stretched under the steering wheel, hot-wiring the ignition, when the owner, who had passed out in the back, loomed over the driver's seat breathing stale beer and shouting for the police. Eddie took off on foot, found a phone, and called Bud to pick him up.

Bud sent Kate along the second time. "Try to get one without the owner inside," he said.

They looked around town until they found another van on Hydraulic Street. This one wasn't even locked and kicked over on the first try.

The Hutchinson job would be number eight in a string of bank holdups the American Patriotic Force had committed. The robberies weren't bringing in much money, but they generated publicity. Kate had followed the articles in the Kansas City paper and had heard that even the East Coast newspapers picked up the story. They were comparing the APF to Pretty Boy Floyd and the Barrow Gang. Some of them even printed Bud's letters, where he claimed the robberies were a protest against banks foreclosing on farmers and auctioning off their equipment and animals.

Bud made the most of the publicity by circulating weekly tape-recorded speeches to keep the faithful in touch with his progress.

"We're freemen," he said on the only one she played through to the end, "not criminals. We rob banks for the same reason we refuse to pay taxes. We're protesting the imposition of the New World Order by alien forces set on destroying the American way of life. We are at the grassroots of a great American Revolution." She'd heard that part of the speech so often when she was a child that she could recite it word for word.

Bud had booked them into a run-down motel near downtown Wichita, and Wayne Griggs was there, cast and all. He'd done the original surveillance. They gathered around the kitchen table in his room for the final briefing.

Griggs kept a cigarette dangling from his lips while he talked. His face combined Appalachian cheekbones with scars from adolescent acne, and he had an almost reptile-slim body. Every time he looked at Kate, he sneered like he knew something dirty about her.

Hutchinson was ideal, he told them, leaning back in his chair with the look of a man who knew it all. The building was old, probably turn of the century. Hutchinson seemed like such a safe town that no one had bothered remodeling it, so there were front and side entrances, both open during business hours, with curbside parking and no security guard.

"And here's the sweet part." Griggs gave Bud the look of a prize scholar waiting for his master's approval. "Some hotshit from North Dakota just bought it out. He's been foreclosing like a sumbitch to make his nut."

Kate remembered a joke Kansas farmers told—that they owed the banker for everything but their wives. The truth was that, with the cost of new equipment, expanded acreage, seed, and fertilizer, most of them were just a season away from bankruptcy.

"They're talking mean." Griggs drew another puff of his cigarette. "People are getting up and walking out of the Hi-Ho Cafe when he comes in for morning coffee."

Bud assembled the squad early so they could get to Hutchinson before the morning shoppers hit the main street. Kate spent the trip huddled by the rear door of the van. Her stomach was unsettled, and she ached with exhaustion. Every bump in the road made her feel more like throwing up.

By the time the van stopped in Hutchinson, she'd calmed down. Outside the rear window, the street was deserted. Even for this time of day, it was too quiet. She opened her mouth to speak just as Bud gave the signal to move out.

She pulled her ski mask down. Eddie pushed the rear door open, and they burst out, running as soon as they hit the ground. They were armed with mean-looking black shotguns with short barrels, Remington 870 riot guns, carrying strung buck loads which could shred anything they hit.

Inside, Delbert, and Eddie shouted, "Stay Calm! Don't move! Quiet." Kate's mouth was too dry to make sounds.

Standing in the entrance, she saw a marble counter with two teller stations. One was closed, and, at the other, a middle-aged woman stood behind decorative brass bars that offered no protection at all. Her customer was a frail man in a suit that might have fit once but hung on him now. Off in the corner, the secretary sat at her desk. The bank president was nowhere in sight.

Kate felt her shoulders relax as she took a deep breath of relief. These people were not going to put up a fight. This would be a quick in and out.

The teller looked straight at Kate, her mouth open in a silent scream, as Delbert moved toward her. The customer didn't notice a thing. He leaned intently toward the teller's cage and kept right on talking.

"So why don't I get six and a half percent?" he asked in the loud voice of someone who doesn't hear well. To emphasize his point, he tapped the counter with a skinny index finger.

Kate felt herself wince when Delbert shoved the old man aside and rested the short barrel of his weapon on the edge of the counter.

"Don't throw the panic switch, not with your hands, not with your feet. Understand?"

The woman nodded. The color had drained out of her face, leaving it so grey that she looked like her heart would stop any minute.

Eddie waited by the gate-like door that marked the entrance to the area behind the teller's cages. The door was controlled by a buzzer at the teller's station. On Delbert's nod, the teller pushed the button allowing it to swing open.

Kate slipped toward the president's desk, which was gleaming in the morning sun. His secretary sat in front of a computer terminal. The Plexiglas nameplate on her desk read Viola McKinnon. She was a plump woman wearing a boxy blue suit, which she'd attempted to soften with a lacy white blouse. She looked up at Kate with a confused, half-formed smile frozen on her face.

From the corner of her eye, Kate saw Eddie enter the work area behind the teller's window and pull a canvas bag from under his coat.

"Open up those cash drawers and fill his bag." Delbert said in the voice of a man who was in no hurry. "Make sure you don't give him any marked bills." He paused, looking around, then turned his attention back to the teller. "We know where you live."

"It's not my money," the teller said. Her voice had the reedy quality of choked fear.

"You just keep that in mind," Delbert said.

Kate thought she ought to herd the customer over with the secretary, but the old man stood quietly beside Delbert, studying him with the puzzled expression of someone verging on making sense of a string of dream images. The secretary was still seated with her hands on the edge of her desk. Kate gestured with the barrel of the shotgun, and she raised them slightly and looked like she wanted to cry.

"I've just been on this job a month," she said. Her voice caught, as if she were suppressing a sob.

"Just stay quiet, and you'll be okay," Kate said softly so Delbert and Eddie wouldn't hear.

29

The woman nodded obediently.

A car started outside the bank, and Kate turned to see the van pulling away. Bud was leaving. This wasn't part of the plan. Just as she turned to call to Delbert, there was a rush of air as the front door flew open, and men dressed in camouflage jumpsuits swarmed into the lobby shouting, "Drop your weapons! Freeze!"

She was moving toward the side exit door when the first round of gunfire exploded. Eddie vanished behind the teller's counter, and Delbert spun toward her. The black mask covered most of his face, but she could see his eyes darting back and forth like he was scared. He leveled his gun in her direction. She raised her arms to stop him, but as she did, he fired.

Kate stepped back. For a moment she thought she'd been hit but when she looked at herself she saw no bullet holes, felt no pain. She turned toward the door and saw Viola McKinnon crumpled against the wall like a broken doll, blood spurting from her neck and chest, spattering the area around her with red specks. Her mouth was moving, as if she were struggling to speak. After a second Kate dropped her shotgun and went to her, wrapping her arms around her, hugging her tightly, as if that could plug up the holes. There was a terrible odor of urine and shit along with the metallic scent of gunpowder. Kate realized she was smelling death and let go.

Gunshots came from several directions. Kate looked up to see Delbert's body being blown forward, arms spread out as if he'd taken flight. In the middle of it all, the old man stood weaving uncertainly, untouched but buffeted by the sound of the gunfire.

Kate headed for the side door. Gruber told her later that one of the deputies had been assigned to block that exit but at the first gunshot he dove under a desk and didn't come out until the shooting stopped.

Hurling herself into the street, she saw two sheriffs' cars parked to block traffic in either direction. The van was nowhere in sight.

She felt strangely calm, almost like someone had slowed everything to half speed. A paunchy man in a black sweatshirt stood in her path, making to grab her. He caught her by one arm, but she pulled back enough to land a solid kick to his kneecap and heard it crunch under her boot. The man grunted with pain and loosened his grip just enough for her to pull free. She yanked her ski mask off and threw it aside to give herself full range of vision.

She heard the shouts and footsteps of people chasing her as she rounded the street corner. Someone may have even fired a shot at her—she wasn't sure. Her breath came in short, raspy spurts and tore at her chest. Still running, she ducked into a Ben Franklin store and cut through the cluttered aisles, past an astonished sales clerk and into the storeroom in the back, where she pushed past a skinny man in a UPS uniform standing by a wooden crate with a clipboard in his hand. Someone was shouting, "Police! Stop."

Outside, she ran down an alley, through a used car lot, then across an empty schoolyard, cutting from the swings to the slide, past the monkey bars. She thought she heard children singing, but it must have been her own hoarse breathing because the windows were closed to the February wind.

She had no idea where she was going. For all she knew, she could have been heading straight toward the sheriff's office. She went through yards, over fences, hearing sirens from all directions, but no law officers appeared in front of her. She found an open garage and crouched in one corner on a dirt floor, waiting to catch her breath. Any minute they'd show up and take her away.

She sat so quietly that her arms and legs went numb, and her mind went dead, as if someone had thrown a switch, cutting off all thought. She could only sit in a corner, watching motes of dust in the winter sun.

There was no reason why she should have gotten away. Delbert was dead. If Eddie was alive, he'd talk. At survival camp, she'd learned that sooner or later everyone talks. And Bud was gone. Something had alerted him, and he'd driven off. The general had abandoned his troops.

Kate reviewed her choices. She could sit and wait to be found, or she could stand up, walk herself into the sheriff's office and surrender. Or she could try to make it to the Ditton place.

Crouched there in the dirt, she kept on breathing heavily long after her body should have been rested. She breathed so fast her toes and fingers tingled with hyperventilation until she forced herself to take slow, measured breaths, counting from one on the inhale to ten on the exhale. A cold wind blew through cracks in the garage, and the dirt floor was hard. Her left leg fell asleep. She shifted her position; it felt as if red-hot needles were poking in and out. She rubbed it to restore circulation and, for an instant, felt the weight of the dead woman's body against her again.

She hid until the angle of the winter sun through the dirty panes told her it was late afternoon. Pulling herself off the floor, she pushed open the door to peek out at an empty backyard and the back porch of a tiny house. There was no movement from inside, and no heads appeared at a window to look out. She moved out slowly, weaving through backyards, meeting only a puzzled-looking mongrel in one yard and a frenzied poodle in another. She worked her way to the edge of town, then stopped and oriented herself. The Ditton place was fifteen miles north of town. Someone must have talked by now and the sheriff would know where she was going. The deputies would have all the time they needed to get there and meet her. Still, that had been the plan. Finish the plan, she told herself. She'd get to the farm, deputies would be waiting, and it would all be over.

The west wind picked up at sundown and sliced through her army surplus jacket. The moon was full and icy white. Sometimes she imagined herself running into a barrage of gunfire at the Ditton place. Other times she simply raised her hands in surrender, ready to face whatever punishment fell on her. She ran until she lost her breath, then walked, then trotted, but she kept moving all through the night. As long as she could keep moving, she didn't have to see Viola McKinnon's body in front of her.

Toward morning, she stopped at a stock tank and, breaking a film of ice off the top, bent forward to suck the cold, clear water. It tasted sweet, and she drank for a long time, reminding herself it might be the last water she ever tasted.

The three buildings and one tree at the Ditton place were the only visible breaks in the flat prairie horizon. There were no cars around, but that didn't mean anything. She looked for fresh tracks as she approached, but didn't see any. If they were staking her out, they'd done a good job. She moved cautiously, hoping some hotshot wouldn't just pick her off with a sniper's rifle, and she kept her hands visible, ready to raise them at the first sign of movement.

She reached the house and looked in a window at an empty living room with peeling wallpaper and a floor littered with newspapers. A tiny fire truck lay on the windowsill, waiting for someone to play with it. She stared at it for a long time, feeling half-sick.

She turned away from the house and moved slowly and resolutely toward the shed. She hesitated a second at the door, then said, "Fuck it," and pulled the hasp open, sliding the battered door to one side. Sunlight hit the fenders of a white '79 Dodge pickup. Beside it in the shadows stood a faded green Chevy of the same year. Kate let her eyes adjust to the gloom. No one jumped from behind either of them. The door groaned as the wind rocked it, but that was the only sound.

Kate opened the Chevy and got in. The keys were in the ignition. When she reached for them, her hands were shaking, so she sat awhile, calming herself. She drove straight west, stopping only for coffee and gas. Her eyes felt gritty, and her legs ached with exhaustion. She bought a sandwich at Hays, Kansas, because she thought she should eat something, but the sight of it brought back the queasiness of the morning, and she tossed it on the roadside for a coyote to find.

She drove all the way to Pueblo, Colorado, before she stopped to sleep. By that time, her vision was blurring so badly she was having trouble seeing the road, and visions of the dead woman kept popping up off the blacktop. She slept for four hours, then dragged herself into a truckstop for breakfast. Someone had left a copy of the *Denver Post* on the lunch counter. The robbery had claimed space on the front page. There'd been a tip-off. Deputies had been waiting and struck when they spotted a stolen van in front of the bank. Kate rested the paper on the counter and stared off into the distance. She remembered Griggs and his nasty little smile. If he was the rat, he'd better hide good, because Bud wouldn't stop until he got him.

She picked the paper up again. There were photos of her father and of her. Bud was in battle dress uniform. Her picture had been taken for her graduation from Tascosa High School in Amarillo. The article said she was missing from her classes at the University of Kansas and was presumed to have been involved with the robbery.

Kate looked at her picture as if she were seeing her face for the first time. She compared the photo to her reflection in the mirror behind the counter. No one would ever confuse her with the confident, hopeful young woman in the newspaper. Her hair was greasy with sweat and dust, her face was drawn, and her eyes were dark with exhaustion.

There were other pictures: the bank president looking haggard, an old photo of the secretary, Viola McKinnon, taken at a family party. She looked up at the camera, smiling with surprise. Her funeral would be held in Hutchinson but the body would be buried in the family plot at Greensburg, Kansas.

The bus hit a bad stretch of highway as Kate remembered all this, and the baby across the aisle fussed until its mother could arrange herself to nurse. Greensburg came up fast, just after Pratt. The bus made a boxy turn off the road and pulled up at a truckstop by the side of Highway 54. The cashier directed her to the cemetery and offered to watch her bags while she walked there.

Greensburg was a dusty, angular town of frame houses and trees that had been whipped by the western wind until they all pointed east. Fading signs advertised the world's deepest well. Kate wondered how they knew for sure.

The cemetery stood at the end of a paved street, unconnected to any church building. Kate wandered from plot to plot, unexpectedly fascinated by the names and dates until an old man in overalls stopped by in his pickup and asked if she needed help. She hesitated, afraid he'd want to know why she was asking for the McKinnon plot, but she told herself she could be a niece or cousin. She gave him the name, and he directed her to row thirty-seven, plot three.

The plot held a large granite tombstone surrounded by smaller, flat stones marking the bodies of various McKinnons—Elmer, Hazel, Edna Mae, wife of Leonard, and, finally, Viola (1934-1982), "Taken before her time." Someone had put vases of plastic flowers by each marker, and they swayed back and forth in a wind that would have snapped real flowers off their stalks. Kate knelt by the stone, and the force of the wind made her jacket flap angrily at her sides. She'd had a long time to rehearse what she wanted to say here. First in the Sedgwick County jail and then in the Federal Womens' Detention Center, she'd wept for this woman. But the tears were gone now. They hadn't helped Viola McKinnon then and wouldn't help her now.

"I'm going to get him," she said to the stone, nodding to seal the promise. She stretched her hand to trace the letters on the stone as if that could send her words to the dead woman. Then she rose, buttoned her jacket, and wondered if anyone else still visited this spot. Then she turned into the wind to retrace her steps to the highway.

CHAPTER FIVE

Kate got to Amarillo too early for the bank to be open. Although the sun was bright, a cold wind blew in from the west and cut right through her jacket. She stood on Polk Street, in the center of what had once been the main drag. When she was a little girl, the fanciest stores in the tri-state area lined this street—White & Kirk's, Blackburn's, Colbert's—and on weekends every parking space was full of pickups from western Kansas, Oklahoma and New Mexico.

But, at this moment, she couldn't see another person in any direction. The wind whipped a forlorn newspaper at her feet, and the street was so vacant she half expected to see tumbleweeds blowing on the pavement. Polk Street had become a dismal collection of vacant storefronts and abandoned buildings that left it looking like a plague had struck.

Kate was the first customer through the doors when the bank opened at nine-thirty, and she couldn't help looking the place over with a professional eye. The building was old, but it had been remodeled to lower the ceilings with soundproof tile. Instead of tellers cages, there were faux marble counters and not a guard in sight. But a bank this size would have cameras linked to a command center somewhere in the interior of the building, and the tellers would have silent alarms connected to the nearest police station.

The first person she saw was a woman staring into the screen of a computer terminal. The logical thing to do was to walk up and ask who to see about a trust, but she had trouble making herself step up to the desk. She felt she would trigger a silent alarm of her own, one linked to her father and the APF. The action would start, and there

36

would be no backing out.

Still, it had to be done. Just then the woman looked up at her.

"I'd like to talk to someone about collecting a bequest," Kate said.

"You want Mr. Bostwick." The woman pointed at an office on the far side of the room.

Mr. Bostwick was the kind of man who sang in the choir at his Baptist church and mopped sweat from his brow after each number, winter and summer. He wore his thin brown hair exactly the way his mother must have parted and plastered it for him when he was four. His white shirt, navy blue suit and maroon tie combined with a trained smile to assure customers he was the kind of man they could trust with their money.

Mr. Bostwick was happy to meet Kate Porter after all these years—very happy. He stood up to greet her and pumped her hand. As he got close, Kate caught a whiff of talcum powder.

"We've been looking forward to hearing from you, Miz Porter."

He bustled to his desk and fumbled through files until he found the one he wanted. He paused for a moment over the letter she'd sent from Lexington. The envelope was stapled to the back, and she could see the large, black-stamped message that it had been posted at a federal correctional facility. He looked up at her with a smile that said he would love to hear the whole sordid story.

Without being asked, Kate took a chair.

"I'm sorry I couldn't get down to see you. I've been a little busy these past few years." She kept her voice flat and ordered her muscles not to return his smile. The man reminded her of a cat that rubbed itself against you if you refused to pet it. He just wouldn't stop.

Mr. Bostwick looked flustered.

"We have a few forms for you to fill out."

Mr. Bostwick continued to fret while Kate signed forms written in a type size never intended to be read.

"You sure you don't want some traveler's checks?" he asked. That was after Kate had assured him that she wasn't interested in a money-market checking account or a cash card with instant withdrawal privileges. She smiled at him gently and suppressed an urge to lean forward, touch his arm, and tell him that it was all right to accept the cash her father or one of his people had given him. He'd done his job and kept an eye on the Porter trust account. Now he should go ahead and call the number they'd left for him.

The wind was up by the time she left the bank. Kate walked till she found a cafe where she could get biscuits and grits and a copy of the *Amarillo Globe-News*. She settled into a booth next to the unwashed window and kept one eye on the street outside while she searched the paper for used car dealers. Lone Star Used Cars had a half-page ad, a quarter of which was taken up by a photo of the owner, Jesse Kingsley. Ol' Jess had been a hanger-on in the early days, and she was willing to bet he still stayed in touch with the boys in the APF.

After she ate, she called a cab and had it drop her at Lone Star Used Cars, right under a twenty-four-foot photo of Jesse, still grinning.

Kate poked around the cars, looking in the windows and kicking at the tires until she caught the attention of the man himself. Jesse'd put on weight, and his hair had one of the worst comb-overs she'd ever seen. It took him a minute or two to recognize her, and, when he did, the professional smile faded a little. Maybe he was afraid she was going to hit him up for a loan.

"I've got cash money, and I want a pickup," she told him. "Something nice and clean, none of those rolled-back speedometers."

She gestured toward the cars on the lot as if she'd checked them all and had seen the evidence.

Jesse raised his eyebrows conspiratorially.

"Now you know we don't do that here. I got me a new Chevy Six over here. You take it out for a spin and come back in here, and we'll talk price."

Kate poked around the Chevy, the Ford next to it, and the Dodge on down the line. She took the Chevy out for a test. The brakes needed work and the front end felt soft, and when she pushed the gas pedal to the floor, she saw a puff of black smoke through the side mirror, but it would get her where she wanted to go.

The sticker price was a thousand dollars. Jesse was so surprised when Kate didn't dicker that he knocked off a hundred out of habit. A half-hour later, the papers were ready. On her way out the door, she spotted a white Jeep Cherokee that had pulled up alongside the stock-tank dealer across from the used car lot.

She was too far away to get a good look at the man behind the wheel, but his shape was familiar: Lloyd Hughes, a small thin man with sharp cheekbones and a brooding nose. His hair had gone from almost too black to a soapy grey. Good ol' Jesse must have made a quick call while she was waiting for the paperwork.

Back in the old days, Lloyd had been head of security, a position Bud created to keep him happy. Lloyd had applied to every uniformed law enforcement agency in Texas—the Texas Rangers, the Highway Patrol, the sheriff's department, the Amarillo Police Department, even Potter County Animal Control. Every one had refused him. He was too small and too strange.

Lloyd had supervised marksmanship training at one point. Kate recalled his voice at her shoulder, encouraging her to relax into her weapon and squeeze the trigger gently but firmly. Bud said Lloyd had the makings of a gifted sniper. Behind his back, Dwight had called him a slimy little backshooter. Kate suspected they were both right.

Kate forced herself to walk to her truck as if she'd noticed nothing. Lloyd hated informers as much as he loved Bud. Kate tried swallowing but found her mouth had gone unexpectedly dry. If he was going to take her out, he could do it right now. One easy shot. If he timed it right, the noise would be muffled by passing traffic. She'd drop, people would come to check, and, by the time anyone knew she was dead, he'd be gone. Just another unexplained death. Happens all the time.

But no shot came. It was possible her plan would actually work, and she'd be able to draw her father's interest and get him to surface. On the other hand, maybe he'd ordered Lloyd to keep an eye on her so he could take care of her himself.

CHAPTER SIX

Kate figured that if Lloyd wanted to shoot her he would have done it. There were a few things she wanted to take care of before she left, so she decided to let him waste his time following her around. She wanted to drive over to the old house—the place she'd grown up—just to see if it still looked the same.

She eased to the curb across the street, killed the engine, and rolled down the window as if it would give her a clearer view of the second floor window and what had once been her room. The last time she'd seen the place, there'd been a large willow tree in the front yard which sheltered and cooled the house in the summer heat. Mamaw'd managed to keep it alive, even through the terrible seven-year droughts when water was rationed, and they had to sneak a hose out to water both the tree and her rose garden in the middle of the night. But someone had cut the willow down, leaving the front of the house bare and unprotected. They'd also removed Mamaw's rose arbor, which had guarded the backyard like a magic gate.

That's where Kate and Dwight had been sleeping—in Dwight's new tent, the night Mamaw woke them to say that their mother was dead. She'd carried Kate upstairs, pressing her to her breast, saying, "Your mama's gone home to God," while Dwight shuffled sleepily along behind. As they passed her mother's room, Kate caught a glimpse of her mother's dressing gown flung across the bed and her fancy satin house shoes waiting primly on the floor.

Daddy'd been on the road selling Porter Dryland Plows, so they had to raise him on the CB radio down at Lubbock and tell him to come home. The first thing he did when he got there was have

Mamaw take all of the pictures of Mama and put them away. Three days later, Kate stood by while the ladies from the church cleaned out her mother's closet. The only thing she managed to retrieve was a white linen handkerchief smelling of Chanel No. 22, which she sneaked into her room before it was bagged up with everything else and sent to the Salvation Army.

Kate started having nightmares after that, and Dwight began wetting the bed. They took him from doctor to doctor until one suggested a psychologist. Bud took Dwight's hand, thanked the doctor, and left. That was the last time they talked to anybody about his problem. Every morning Mamaw hung his soiled sheets out to air, and they flapped on the clothesline like white banners advertising his shame.

Dwight made a clubhouse, which he grudgingly let Kate share, underneath the lilac bush behind the garage. They'd go there on hot afternoons while Mamaw took her nap. Dwight brought out his road grader, and they made houses and buildings out of milk cartons. Dwight even let her push his grader and help make a hill outside their town.

"This is our country," he told Kate, "and no one else can live here."

Kate found herself the recipient of impersonal and unexpected kindness and attention. Brother Roy, the assistant minister at Temple Baptist Church, had his wife take her shopping for a new Easter outfit that made her look like a dyed baby chick. Friends' mothers took her to beauty parlors for haircuts and perms. She was asked for lots of weekends and overnights. Back at home, they ate dinner in the kitchen, leaving the dining room dark and vacant. Meals were very quiet that year. She and Dwight sat on the same side of the table as a kind of protection against their father's silence. Bud didn't allow bawling, so when Kate cried, it was alone in the little room on the second floor where no one could hear her.

She was in the fifth grade when the IRS brought suit against The Porter Dryland Plow Company. At first Bud was optimistic. He told Mamaw this was only a test case involving a new ruling. His accountant told them the government didn't have a leg to stand on. Porter would win and kick their pork-eating butts all the way back to

Washington. On Speech Day at Wolflin Elementary School, Kate spoke on taxation without representation and won a standing ovation from the principal and the teachers.

And in the end, Bud did win his case, but by that time Porter Dryland Plow was bankrupt. He moved his office to the garage and spent all his time out there, sorting through papers, becoming even more silent. When Kate slipped in to borrow his adding machine for her math problems, he slid it toward her as if even a nod cost more than he could afford.

Eventually he went on the road, selling anhydrous ammonia tanks. He'd been the kind of man who could sell coal in hell, but his gift seemed to have deserted him. After three months, he came home saying the market had dropped, so he switched to fertilizer spreaders, then to one-step trailer hitches. Mamaw served beans and cornbread more often and enrolled Kate and Dwight in the free lunch program at school, making them promise never to tell their father. She still cooked chicken on Sundays, but the only time they ate pot roast was when company came.

Then Bud met a politician named J. Everetts Haley. Haley was a perennial candidate for public office, the kind who had to form his own party because no one else would endorse him. He'd gotten his start as the last of the segregationists, and, when that failed, reshaped himself into a super-patriot dedicated to protecting his country from communism, Zionism and Trilateralism. Kate smiled, remembering his confusion when she asked him to explain Trilateralism one Sunday at dinner. He cleared his throat and sputtered until he dropped mashed potatoes on his pinstriped suit, but he'd never managed an intelligible response.

Their father began to spend long evenings on the screened-in back porch, reading by lamplight after everyone else was in bed. He converted the garage office to a meeting hall and began holding sessions with small groups of tired-looking men who fixed their eyes on the floor while they smoked cigarettes and listened. Kate often crept in to hear her father's talks, nodding along as he spoke of taxation without representation, a subject on which she felt a proprietary interest. "We need to form a corps of modern-day minutemen and patriots to fight creeping socialism." Then he would lower his voice slightly and talk about secret protocols and foreign committees plotting to undermine the precious American Constitution. He always concluded with the same phrase:

"What this country needs is a second American Revolution."

Kate liked that part a lot. It had an important sound.

When the meetings grew too large for the garage, Bud rented a warehouse on the edge of town. The publisher of the local newspaper joined and ordered his editor to begin carrying a weekly column written by someone in the John Birch Society. About that same time, a rancher named Stevens suggested moving the entire operation to his place out in the Canadian River breaks. Kate and Dwight stayed in town with their grandmother, but they spent weekends at the ranch.

Bud took to dressing in combat fatigues, and he got so military that even a simple phone call was a communiqué. He had as flagpole dug into the front yard and ordered the household to begin each day with a flag raising ceremony. Out on the ranch, he called the staff together for prayer and the issuing of orders of the day. He made Dwight his junior officer and had him dress in fatigues and highly polished paratrooper boots. He expected Kate to work in the office or help in the kitchen. She undercooked the eggs and misfiled all the papers until she was permitted to do what she liked, which was practice on the firing range and plan reconnaissance.

When she was twelve, Kate decided it might be fun to play on a baseball team. She knew Bud regarded athletics as a waste of time for girls so she kept her place on the Roadrunners a secret. On practice days, she told Mamaw she was staying late at school to earn extra credit.

One afternoon while she was playing left field, she saw her father stride across Elwood Park and plant himself behind the backstop at home plate, arms folded across his chest, waiting.

Kate forced herself to take her eyes off her father and concentrate on the game. The batter made a clean, sharp hit and sent a line drive in her direction. She caught the ball even though it struck her glove with enough force to push her backwards and threw it in time for the third baseman to tag the runner and put the other team out.

After that, there was no way of postponing it. Kate trotted slowly toward the bench, certain she had played her last inning. Her father was standing next to the coach, listening intently as the other man pointed in Kate's direction.

As she drew close, her father caught her eye and motioned for her to wait. She pulled herself to attention to prepare herself for the lecture that was bound to come.

Moments later, her father left the coach and came to loom over her. "Your coach says you can hit good, you catch anything they throw at you, and you do what you're told. That true?"

Looking straight ahead, Kate nodded. She stood at attention, as if that might somehow help.

Her father was whispering now. "He says you can run like hell."

Kate nodded again, still looking straight ahead.

Her father moved around in front of her until he filled her view. "When you withhold the truth, you lie. Did you know that, Sister?"

Kate nodded

"You can play," Bud said, "but don't ever lie to me again."

Bud traveled all over the Southwest, speaking to small groups at Legion halls, lodges and churches. He recruited retired military men, angry roustabouts laid off from the oil patch, and workers from the Pantex nuclear plant and the decommissioned air force base. J. Everetts introduced him to another level of member, men who were willing to make large contributions as long as they could stay in the background. They took a name—The American Patriotic Front—and a logo, a circle surrounding a musket crossed over an AR-15 military rifle.

By the time she was in eighth grade, Bud was building a network of militia groups from other states. Kate went to her first summer encampment, spending two weeks in Montana. She shared a tent with a dumpy looking woman whose husband was in federal prison for assassinating a Jewish disc jockey in Cincinnati. Dwight called the woman a martyr but Kate found her self-dramatizing and tedious.

It was at the encampment where she got her introduction to paranoia. Everyone talked about infiltrators, surveillance, government agents, and the black helicopters that were supposed to be gathering to swoop down on them. She learned to assume that all telephones were tapped and that every passing airplane could be a U-2 spy plane sent to monitor peaceful citizen assemblies on behalf of the United Nations.

Once they were back in Texas, Bud lectured them about the dangers the APF faced from the federal agents and communist spies trying to infiltrate the organization. Because they were his children, they could expect to be followed, maybe even picked up and questioned. They should trust no one outside the organization, exercise care in choosing friends, and, above all, never talk to outsiders about the APF.

"We're fighting a war here," he said, "and the enemy's all around us. Remember, it's what you don't see that kills you."

Kate always nodded in agreement when her father conducted one of his lectures, which he now called briefings. She knew better than to disagree with him. But privately she felt lonely and isolated. There were no other girls her age in the movement and very few boys. Outside of her brother, who scarcely had time for her, she had no friends and no one to talk to.

By the time Kate was in high school, Bud had developed a side business in weapons distribution. He shipped equipment stolen from military bases in Oklahoma and Texas to a central arsenal in Arkansas, where it could be distributed to other militia groups. He and J. Everetts started a short-wave broadcast network called "The Voice of Freedom," and a mail-order business distributing audiotapes, books, and surplus military equipment and clothing.

Kate trained with the troops, worked after school pulling orders for the mail-order business and learned to do paste-ups for the monthly newsletter, *The Clarion*. She did her first survival hike when she was fourteen, spending four days living off the land in the caprock canyon country of the High Plains.

By her junior year in high school, she could install a telephone tap and pick a lock. She'd led a squad on a survival weekend when a blue norther descended without warning and forced the squad into a dry

45

gulch where they stayed, covered with earth and sagebrush, until the driving snow stopped and they could build signal fires.

Dwight modeled himself on Bud from the start. He got his sharp-shooter medal at thirteen and became a squad leader—the equivalent of a lieutenant—three years later. He never missed a chance to let Kate know he was being groomed for leadership. She responded by trying to exceed him, becoming better at sharpshooting, weapons assembly and explosive detonation. But nothing made any difference. No matter what she did, she'd never be Bud's son.

The summer after his graduation, Dwight and his best friend, Billy Shoey, started working in the tin storage shed at the edge of the ranch property. At first Kate guessed they were out there reading *Playboy* magazines, but when she overheard them planning test explosions she figured they were fabricating fireworks—homemade salutes—for Bud's birthday. No one thought anything about it, even when Dwight mentioned that someone ought to take out the editor of the Pampa, Texas, *Sun*, an admitted Jew and transplanted New Yorker who'd once worked for some radical paper called *Newsday*. Bud had been furious about him because he'd written an editorial calling the APF the "weekend warriors of the lunatic fringe."

The Saturday before Valentine's Day, Billy and Dwight were work-ing in the shed. Dwight left to get a couple of Cokes while Billy fin-ished assembling a circuit. Poor Billy had never been a good reader, and they figured out later he must have read the manual wrong and connected the black wire to the positive terminal. The explosion turned the night sky white, cracking every window on the place, even shattering the mirror over Kate's bed in the bunkhouse. Dwight was found in back of the kitchen, bleeding and unable to move his legs. A sliver of tin had severed his spine just below the eighth cervical nerve. Nothing was found of Billy except one end of his little finger.

Dwight was taken to Northwest Texas Hospital, where he lay, day after day, looking out the window at a blank Texas sky. Bud took care of Billy's funeral and sent his mother on a two-week all-expenses-paid vacation to see her sister in Abilene. When the Potter County deputies inquired, they were told the boys had been making firecrackers and accidentally ignited the barrels of gasoline someone had stored in the shed.

Dwight's girlfriend, Kimberly, visited him three or four times before he asked her not to come back. Bud came every day for the first week but the sight of his son at the mercy of nurses and doctors overcame him. The APF drew him away and soon only Kate came every day after school. She sat beside the bed, sometimes doing homework, sometimes watching TV, sometimes reading aloud, first from the local papers, then mysteries, and, finally, at Dwight's request, from the Bible.

One day she picked up the Gideon Bible from his table and began reading where it fell open, in the Book of Psalms:

"I am like a pelican of the wilderness. I am like an owl of the desert. I watch and am as a sparrow alone up on the housetop."

Dwight usually closed his eyes when she read, but now he turned his head toward her. "Read that again."

When she did, he looked at her so long and hard that she got scared. She wanted to throw the Bible aside and run out the door to get away from the sickening mix of antiseptic and body waste that permeated the room. She wanted to be out in the fresh air and run to someplace where nobody knew her.

"That's what we are, Katie. That's what he did to us. He's turned us into something that doesn't even know its own home."

The words stayed with her for a long time. At school and out at the ranch, she found herself looking at the people like she was separated from them by a glass wall. She was alone, cut off, and at times she found herself gasping for breath just like someone had pumped all the air out of her cage.

Eighteen months later, after physical therapy had given him the torso of an athlete, Dwight announced that he'd been called to the ministry and wanted to go to Bob Jones University.

"There's a place for you with us, son," Bud said once or twice, but when he let it drop, Kate knew he was relieved that Dwight wouldn't be returning. Even though he considered preachers a bunch of pansy-faced parasites, keeping a crippled son around where everyone could see him was bad for APF morale.

That spring, Kate started reading college brochures in the library. Her grades were good, and she'd done well on her SATs. Bud announced she should apply to Texas A&M or Texas Tech to study nursing, or, if she was good at it, medicine.

"Women make good docs," he said.

But Kate was thinking of places farther away—Oberlin, Antioch, Berkeley, even Smith College or Brown University—someplace where she could make a new life for herself. She'd major in natural science, maybe something like cell biology, and she'd live in a dorm where she could have friends and maybe even date someone. She knew her father would never let her go to any of the places she dreamed about because he believed they were cesspools of communism, so she scaled down her dream and applied to the University of Kansas.

Bud was surprised. "Texas not good enough for you?"

"It's just fine, sir, but I thought we might make some useful contacts if I went to school out of state."

"How 'bout Oklahoma, then?"

"Their pre-med program's not as good."

Bud nodded curtly. He agreed to let her skip summer encampment so she could bone up on Latin, and she began to hope there might be a way out. Maybe she could drift away before anyone noticed she was gone.

A door slammed somewhere exciting a small dog to a frenzy of high-pitched barks and bringing Kate back to the present. Then a woman appeared on her front steps, stopping to peer at Kate. Looking in her side mirror, Kate saw a white Jeep Cherokee parked half a block behind her. Lloyd Hughes was behind the wheel, his eyes covered with a pair of mirror shades that were glaring at her like the eyes of a giant insect.

It was time to go.

CHAPTER SEVEN

The Jeep followed discreetly behind while she tried to find her way to the mall. Amarillo had changed, and she got lost trying to follow Georgia Avenue west. Lloyd was probably back there thinking she was trying to lose him.

Once inside the mall she was hit by the competing smells of fried food from the food court, perfume samples and chocolate. It all made her a little queasy. The shops didn't help—they all seemed to scream at her to buy, try, sample, spend. She passed a department store mannequin, artificially thin, posed with one arm raised, as if it were hailing a cab or waving to a distant friend. It had a wig of long red hair framing the face and the plastic smile was almost right. Lissa McEvoy used to raise her arm at just that angle to throw her a wave as she passed the laundry on her way to the strawberry fields back at Lexington.

A woman bumped into her, breaking the reverie. She moved on to another store where reduced-price clothes covered sale tables. Stopping a saleswoman, she got directions to women's dresses. Then she browsed around until she found just the right dowdy dress. Her years on the run had taught her that the best disguise was as a middle-aged woman. She'd once stood in line at the post office directly across from a wanted poster with her own picture on it and gone unrecognized because she'd been just one more plain-looking woman in a polyester pantsuit.

She chose a dress—the kind of thing you'd throw on to go to the office on a day when you didn't feel good. In the dressing room, she slipped it on over her clothes. The hem was about right. It was two sizes too large, but that was okay. She might need the extra space.

In the shoe department she found a pair of black pumps with sensible heels. Next she added a purse big enough to hold a Walther PK with six reloads and still have room for lunch and a change of underwear.

The last stop was the wig department, where she tried on Raquel Welch specials until she found one that made her look fifteen years out of date. The dress would add a good twenty pounds, and, with some careful make-up, she'd easily pass for forty-five.

Her last stop was the luggage department, where she found a navy blue duffel bag. She paid cash for it and took her bags to the women's room so she could fold the shopping bag on the bottom of the duffel with the shoes, dress, purse, and wig on the top. She paused for a moment, wondering whether to buy underwear but decided a pair of pantyhose would do. On second thought, she'd make that two pair, just in case.

The white Cherokee wasn't in sight when she loaded her bags in the pickup, but when she left the mall parking area, it moved in two cars behind her. She drove to a Copper Kettle restaurant, taking care to park toward the back, behind a dumpster, so she couldn't be seen from the road.

She found a booth by a window, which gave her a view of the parking lot while she drank coffee and studied the menu. The white Cherokee had pulled into the parking lot of the Steak-Inn Restaurant next door.

When the waitress came by, Kate asked for a phone and was directed to the hallway outside the men's room. She dropped a quarter in and dialed 911.

"I'm at the Copper Kettle on Georgia," she said. "There's a Jeep Cherokee at the Steak-Inn parking lot, and a man is standing in the back with no pants on."

"No pants," the operator repeated.

"That's right. He's wearing a shirt, but he's got no pants and no drawers. He'd just standing there waving his weenie in the wind."

Kate hung up before the operator could ask for her name and number. She waited till an Amarillo Police Department car drove up, then she slid out of her booth, leaving five dollars for the waitress. Lloyd Hughes was standing alongside the police car, gesturing broadly, when she left.

Kate called Gruber when she got to Tulia, Texas. "We're in business," she said. "Any change in plan?"

Gruber said things were great. "If you want to see blue herons," he said, "meet me in San Antone Tuesday afternoon. They'll be everywhere."

CHAPTER EIGHT

South of Tulia the road got empty and flatter. It was going to be a long night. Lloyd Hughes would have gotten on the horn and the CB to call out every good old boy in northwest Texas. This was the APF's home country, and deputies or even the state highway patrol might be on the lookout for her. Still, it would be hard for anyone to ambush her on a road this quiet.

She ran through the plan over and over to distract herself from the monotony of Texas ranch country. She'd surfaced in Amarillo, attracted her father's attention, then vanished. So far so good. By now Bud should be wondering what she was up to, and somebody would figure she'd left Amarillo. They'd be checking the highways and sooner or later they'd find her driving south. This was the part that made Gruber nervous. They might decide she was dangerous and take her out right then and there. But Kate had a hunch they'd follow her to see what she was doing. Then she'd vanish again. That ought to make Bud really edgy and, if it worked, drive him to surface wherever he was holed up. He'd want to do things right, and that meant he'd come looking for her in person.

"Its like hunting jackrabbits," she'd told Gruber. "First you see them, then you don't. Makes you so mad you'll never give up till you get them."

Except the them was a her, and the fact was, the hunter usually got the jackrabbit.

In a molten red West Texas sunset just outside Matador she noticed a Ford Expedition hanging back, matching her speed. She couldn't make out more than one person inside, so if he was going to make a move he'd have to pass her, then force her to stop.Or he might be in contact with someone ahead. In that case, they'd pick a deserted stretch, try to drive her off the road and finish her right there.

She kept one eye on the rearview mirror, but after awhile, when nothing happened, she relaxed a little. She looked up at the stars, wishing she had someone to show them to. At Lexington privacy was scarce, and she'd craved time alone. But now, driving across this empty land, she felt deeply and horribly lonely. She fiddled with the radio, trying to find some jazz but all she got was the Judds singing "Born to Be Blue."

Somebody had been blasting the Judds on her first day in the laundry at Lexington. Laundry detail was supposed to be the worst job in the place—wet cement floors that made your feet ache, hot steam in the summer, and detergents that ate the skin right off your hands. Kate volunteered as soon as she heard about it.

They put her on the sort line, handling clothes from hospitals, jails and institutions—shit-stained pajamas, blood-spattered scrubs, and O.R. drapes, greasy aprons and shirts. She had gloves to keep out body fluids, but they didn't help with the stench.

She worked with two other women—one, Shabeeka from Detroit, was doing ten to fifteen for helping her boyfriend rob a mail truck. She gave Kate a snort that said don't mess with me and turned away to a running conversation with her friends pushing loads of wet wash. Tracy, the other woman, had wide-set eyes behind eyeglasses with cracked lenses and frames, giving her the look of someone who was always three steps behind. She didn't talk much—just swayed back and forth while she worked, listening to music inside her head.

Kate had already heard about Tracy. She was in for kidnapping a nine-month-old baby from its stroller. She didn't feed it, and the baby died. Her lawyer said she was retarded, but the jury didn't care—she was in Lexington for the rest of her life.

Kate told herself the blood wouldn't get to her. When she flashed back to the Hutchinson State Bank, she stopped herself before she got to Viola McKinnon's body in her arms. She recited her college roommate's haiku, tried to remember the lyrics to "Muskrat Love" by the

Captain and Tenille and reconstructed nursery rhymes she didn't know she remembered.

Jack be nimble, Jack be quick, Jack! Jack! Jack!—

She couldn't get the next line.

"Goddamn it," she said. It must have been loud because Shabeeka stopped trading insults with a woman pushing an empty cart and stared at her.

She started again, this time whispering the words to herself: "Jack be nimble, Jack be—" She stopped. All she could do was stare down at the blood-spattered scrub shirt in her hands. Even through rubber gloves, it felt damp and sticky, like the jacket of Viola McKinnon's little blue suit.

Her hands were shaking. She made a fist to get control, but then her knees felt like they were giving out. She clutched the edge of the worktable to steady herself, but her feet slid out from under her, and she fell to the floor, gasping for breath, then sobbing uncontrollably. She clutched her stomach like she could cut the air off and stop herself. Then she pounded the concrete floor with her fists, even after she tore the rubber gloves and bled on the concrete.

Someone knelt beside her and put an arm over her shoulder. Then the shift boss loomed over, yelling at everyone to get back to work. Tracy was on the floor beside her, offering her work apron for Kate to dry her eyes. Someone else handed her a Kleenex and helped her to her feet.

Except for the sound of the washers and the clothes tumbling in the dryers, the laundry had fallen silent. Kate kept her eyes down. She couldn't look up and see them all watching her.

They made her go talk to the social worker. But Kate insisted she didn't want to change jobs. The laundry was where she belonged.

After she'd been back awhile, Shabeeka decided she might be worth talking to. Shabeeka let it be known that she was on the sort line by choice. She had, she announced, business to take care of. Kate noticed her searching certain shipments, saw her pocketing plastic baggies from time to time. She must have overlooked one, because Kate noticed a lump inside a pair of work pants. She reached in the pocket and pulled out a baggie stuffed with tiny Saran Wrap packages of white powder. Kate pocketed the bag and slipped it to Shabeeka at break.

Shabeeka looked at her suspiciously. "You take any?"

Kate shook her head, and Shabeeka looked surprised. On afternoon break she joined Tracy and Kate as they squatted against a wall. She handed Kate a Snickers bar. "I bet you do these."

Kate gave her a little smile and broke the bar into three pieces.

She killed the radio and let the sound of the wind roaring though an open window keep her company. Tracy was dead—viral pneumonia left untreated. Shabeeka was gone too—she bought it in a crossfire eight months out of the gate.

"Goddamn, I miss you girls," Kate said aloud.

Old-timers said they always got scared and lonely after they got out. She hadn't believed them then—but she did now.

CHAPTER NINE

The Explorer fell away and was replaced by a dark Silverado at the town of Snyder. It, too, kept a steady distance behind Kate, slowing when she slowed, picking up speed when she floored the pickup. From time to time the driver flashed his headlights, like he was winking at her—daring her to stop and slug it out. The fucker was playing with her.

A white reflecting sign announced that she was entering the town of Robert Lee. It wasn't the kind of place you'd even bother to slow down in, but Kate dropped her speed anyway, just to be careful. It looked like every household in town had gone to bed, leaving the place lit by a solitary street lamp and a forlorn front porch light burning for someone who probably wouldn't show up.

She checked her rearview mirror, but there were no headlights following. She slowed for a few miles, waiting to see if the Silverado would catch up, but no headlights appeared. She fidgeted in her seat, trying to figure out what to do next. She could just hit it and burn rubber all the way to Waco. Or she could pull off and wait to see what was going on.

She drove along to the side of the road until she spotted a track that looked promising. Off the highway, she killed her lights and drove by starlight and instinct until she was out of sight. She turned off the engine and left the truck, taking care to shut the door softly. She walked back to a rise where she had a view of the highway. Then she waited. She was taking a risk. If they turned in, she'd have to make a run for it. Her only hope would be to dodge around in the breaks and gulleys until she outran them, but she wanted to know what was going on.

A pair of headlights appeared on the highway, slowed, and then moved on, only to reappear a few minutes later. They'd be using night vision scopes, which would pick up the heat emissions from the engine and her own body and outline them like a red photo. If they wanted her, they had her, but the headlights only paused a moment, then picked up speed. They were following her all right, but their job was surveillance, not murder.

She shivered, then stretched in the night air to shake the tension from her shoulders. She looked up to follow a passing satellite as it arced across the sky. A coyote or two would have made the scene perfect, but the night was quiet. Suddenly she felt cold all the way through to her bones. She returned to the truck and turned on the heater full blast, filling the cab with dry, warm air.

By the time she got to Waco, the Silverado had been replaced by a GMC Jimmy. Kate pulled into a gas station and took time refueling and paying so she could get a look at the passengers. It was hard to see them in the thin, early morning light, but she made out two large men in western hats, both with the look of linebackers gone to fat.

She led them into Waco, driving around and around, snatching glances at the map folded open on the seat beside her while she tried to find the center of town. She figured she'd find the bus depot somewhere downtown. She was starting to feel confident, almost cocky. If they wanted to try to keep up with her, they'd have to work at it.

She led them to a parking lot near the bus depot, and as she removed her suitcase from the passenger seat, she saw the linebackers' Jimmy hovering near an intersection a block away. She took her time going inside and chose the longest ticket line to give them plenty of time to catch up with her.

The linebackers got to the depot just as she got up to the ticket window. She got her first clear look at them. They were dressed nearly identically in dun-colored twills, but they displayed no badges or shields. Still, there was something about the way they surveyed the bus depot as if it were their property that made her think they were police—or at least rental cops.

The taller of the two men paused a moment, then pushed his way in front of the ticket line next to Kate's so he could see where she was headed. As she left the window, she heard him asking which door the bus for Lubbock left from.

Kate took her place in line behind a family of impassive Mexican Indians. Both linebackers were marching in her direction as she prepared to board. A baggage handler with a flatbed cart cut through the line, momentarily cutting off her pursuers. Kate pushed against the woman in front of her, then bolted and ran between parked buses, out a long parking lot and through an alley lined with dumpsters overflowing with plastic garbage bags.

She made her way around a corner and down another alley until she came to an intersection with a taxi stand. One cab was parked in the shade of a building, the driver dozing behind the wheel. Kate woke him when she slammed into the back seat and asked to be taken to the airport. As the cab pulled away, she turned to look out the rear window. No one was following, but that didn't mean a thing. If they were as good as she thought they were, they'd watch every exit from town.

She'd bought a ticket for Houston and was in the departure lounge for American Eagle by the time the linebackers caught up with her. This time they posted themselves at either end of the waiting area, blocking both exits.

A plane landed, and a party of elderly women flocked to the ladies' room. Kate slid herself into the middle of the group and then pushed past them in time to seize a rear stall. While the women chattered and complained about tiny seats, a bumpy ride and poor food, Kate rested her suitcase on the toilet seat and opened it, pulling out the dress, the pumps and the wig. After slipping out of her own clothes, she wiggled into the pantyhose, pulled the dress on over her head, and put on her new shoes.

Next she collapsed the duffel and stashed it at the bottom of the shopping bag, folding her old clothes on top. Standing between the narrow metal walls of the toilet stall, she looked at her possessions for a moment. She'd feel better when she had a new pair of jeans.

The make-up was harder. She'd never been good at it, but she stood at the mirror laying on foundation, darkening her eyebrows, thickening lashes until she looked like a newcomer to Mary Kay.

She was gathering herself, checking zippers and hemlines, when an elderly lady emerged from the toilets looking confused.

"Can I help you?" Kate's voice was now pure Texas matron.

The woman squinted and turned her good ear closer to Kate.

"Let me help you to the door, Mama," Kate said, offering to take the woman's shopping bag. The woman smiled as she strained to make out Kate's words, but she offered her shopping bag and took Kate's arm.

Kate emerged from the bathroom as the overprotective daughter of an elderly woman, burdened with both her mother and two enormous shopping bags, and together they walked past one of the linebackers and down to the arrivals area. She turned the old woman over to a baggage handler and got herself a cab.

She changed cabs three times. The second driver, anxious to make a buck, offered to drive her out to the site of the Branch Davidian compound.

"You can see right where they all fried," he said.

"Just take me to the Marriott," she said.

She phoned for another cab to take her to the Holiday Inn, where she checked in as Andrea Martin from Matador, Texas, paying cash for a one-night stay.

CHAPTER TEN

Kate took a commuter flight from Dallas to San Antonio and caught an airport bus that was packed with conventioneers coming to a national gathering of barbershop quartets. They were mostly men over sixty, and several of them winked at her. She smiled back, wondering if they could tell she was thinking how great it would feel to slam them into the nearest wall and ask them to sing a chorus or two of "The Old Grey Mare."

Gruber lounged in front of the Bexar County courthouse waiting for her. He told her he'd been inside talking to a couple of deputies he'd met at a peace officers convention.

"They think Bud may have moved on down to Corpus, but I'd still like to interview this woman, some kind of cop hag, who says she might have seen something."

"Something what?" Kate asked.

"I'm going out to Kerrville to find out what."

"I'll come along."

Gruber shook his head but she persisted until he shrugged and led her to his car.

They drove to Kerrville, a town outside San Antonio that looked like it had given itself over to the kind of retirement communities where people called their trailers mobile homes. It took almost an hour of driving past white picket fences with cute little signs announcing the owners' first and last names to reach a decidedly less upscale park where they found number 123 Bluebonnet Lane. The aluminum siding was rusting, and wispy patches of grass struggled to compete with the encroaching weeds, which had already seized the flowerbeds, leaving only a few tired and beaten survivors. A country mailbox perched on a post, its open door revealing several flyers and an assortment of bills. Kate pulled one out to look at it. It was addressed to Mrs. Darlene Edwards.

Gruber knocked twice before a whiskey voice called, "Who is it?"

"Raymond Gruber, ma'am." Kate had never heard him refer to himself by his full name. "I'm a friend of Donald Piersall."

The woman who opened the door wore tight jeans and a tank top that failed to cover a solid roll of fat around her waist. Her hair was a red that only came from bottles, and it framed her face with a square of permed ringlets that were meant to detract from a jutting chin. Her eyebrows were penciled onto her forehead, and her eyes framed with heavy mascara, giving them an ingenuous look that contrasted heavily with the knowing lines around her mouth.

"How do you know Don?" she said.

"I'm with the Kansas Bureau of Investigation." Gruber extended the leather wallet with his badge and identification. "Don said you might help us with an investigation. This is Miss Porter." He gestured toward Kate as if she were a fellow officer—or at least his assistant.

Kate stood awkwardly to one side, painfully aware that her faded jeans, worn running shoes, and T-shirt didn't fit the image of a policewoman. She wished she'd bought some new jeans, even though they wouldn't have helped.

The woman ignored Kate and examined Gruber's badge, squinting to read the print. Then she waved them in to a living room furnished with a couch and two armchairs covered in black and yellow plaid. The floor was carpeted in faded shag that had once been avocado. Beyond, the dining area had a round maple table with four captain's chairs. Looking into the kitchen, Kate saw a sink filled with dishes. The smell of bacon grease hung in the air.

Darlene Edwards motioned for them to sit down. "Can I get you some iced tea?"

Gruber said, "Thank you." Kate merely nodded. She was afraid that if she spoke Darlene Edwards would ask why she was really there.

Gruber relaxed into the plaid sofa and stretched his legs out beside the coffee table. Kate eased herself hesitantly into an armchair across from him. Darlene went to the kitchen and searched for glasses first in one cupboard, then another, apparently with no success, because she began running water to rinse dishes in the sink.

"Did you have trouble finding me?" she called over the sound of the water.

"Not a bit." Gruber smiled at Kate.

She brought their iced tea, heavily sugared. Gruber took a long pull from his and started to set the glass on the coffee table in front of him. Kate caught his eye, and he stopped in mid-air and began searching for a coaster.

"Just set it down anywhere," Darlene laughed. "You want an ashtray, hon?" she asked Kate.

Kate shook her head, but Darlene continued bustling around until she found a huge ashtray, emptied it in the garbage and returned to place it in the center of the table where it sent up a reek of stale ashes. Then she took a seat at the end of the couch, perching on the edge so she could lean closer to Gruber. She took a long drink of tea, lit a cigarette from a pack in front of her, inhaled and began.

"Don must have told you about Johnny Miller."

"Yes, ma'am," Gruber said.

Darlene smiled at him as if she were grateful for his every word.

"I don't want to get him in any trouble," she said.

Gruber explained that they weren't interested in Johnny, only in— and he paused to give his words weight—"his associates."

Darlene smiled again and, in a breathy, pressured voice, told them how she met Johnny at ladies' night at a cowboy bar, how they'd dated, and how she got suspicious because he spent so many weekends away. Johnny had guns—the ones she considered usual—pistols, rifles and shotguns and the more exotic, like automatic rifles and mortars, and some that looked like they might be used to launch something. One had a kind of grenade on one end. He once showed her something he said could take out a tank. Darlene spoke mainly to Gruber, throwing only an occasional glance in Kate's direction to be sure she had her attention.

"How'd you find out he was involved in a militia?" Gruber inserted when she paused for breath.

"He liked wearing his uniform around the house, and there were pictures everywhere—him posed with the boys. He even kept a scrapbook."

"And the other man?"

"Well," she began again with a confident smile, "Johnny and I broke up in—" She groped for the date. "—July. I thought he might be dating that Betty Hinkle," she said as if they would know who she meant. "So I used to drive by his house after work just to see if she was there."

Darlene took a deep drag and looked at Kate as if to say, we both know how men are. Gruber caught her eye and signaled for her to nod.

"I saw a car there one night—I thought it was hers. I'd stopped with the girls after work, so I was a little, you know—" Her voice trailed off.

Gruber and Kate both smiled and nodded. They knew.

"So I went up there. I still had a key. I marched right in because if she was sitting up there with my boyfriend, I was sure going to tell her what a, pardon me, b-i-t-c-h she was."

She stopped and looked apologetically in Kate's direction. "So I get inside, and there's this man in the kitchen. He was an old guy with white hair—kind of skinny. He was wearing military camouflage. Johnny came in and almost had a heart attack right there on the spot. He started yelling at me to get out of there. The old guy told him to shut up. They went in the bedroom, and I heard him saying something about the FBI." Darlene looked up at the ceiling as if she were seeing a video of the evening. "So Johnny hustles me out the front door just hollering—What do I want? Why am I coming in his house? It was like he was crazy or something."

She took a drag off the cigarette drooping between the first two fingers of her right hand. "Or maybe he was scared."

She gave Gruber a significant look as if the story were getting thicker.

"Do you think you could identify the man?" Gruber spoke gently like he was afraid of interrupting her train of thought.

Darlene paused a moment, then nodded.

Gruber extended a photo of Bud. "Does this look anything like him?"

Darlene looked hard at the photo, then reached into a box on the coffee table and extracted her glasses. She put them low on her nose and raised the photo for a second look. "That could be him." She sounded hesitant.

"His eyes," Kate spoke for the first time. "Do you remember his eyes?"

Darlene smiled in recognition. "I sure do. They were blue, real blue like—" She picked up a lighter resting beside her cigarettes and flicked it until a flame appeared. "Like the blue in here."

Gruber thanked her and started to stand up.

"Listen." Darlene touched his arm to restrain him. "I won't be getting Johnny in any trouble, will I? I sure don't want to make him no trouble."

"Absolutely not." Gruber gave her his most trustworthy smile.

"He's not wanted for anything in Kansas, is he?"

"No ma'am, this is just part of an investigation in progress."

"So its all confidential?"

"Absolutely."

Darlene smiled, satisfied. Kate had the feeling that every word of this meeting would be repeated in all the cowboy bars in Kerrville before the night was over.

On the way back, Gruber suggested they go for a beer. They wandered along the Riverwalk, Gruber close by her side, tall, almost protective. It had been years since a man walked next to her for any reason except to guard her. They found a bar decorated to look like a French bistro with a Spanish accent, and Gruber ceremoniously pulled out her chair for her.

They ordered a Pearl for Kate and a mineral water for Gruber. When it arrived, Kate took a slow sip. This was her first cold beer in a long time. When she'd been in Lexington the ever-resourceful Fat Alice dealt a noxious home brew, and, every once in awhile, she managed to get genuine beer smuggled in by a guard, but it had almost never been really cold, just as the showers were almost never really hot.

Gruber stretched back in his chair. "Looks like we've got a good I.D. on the old man here. And I'm thinking that Corpus might be a good bet. He'll hide out there until after the election." She'd never heard her father spoken of that way before. Gruber grinned like a man with a full house.

"Why Corpus?"

Gruber leaned across the table and lowered his voice. "What they got there are big-time weapons shipments. The place is stuffed full of military bases. They even got a factory manufacturing land mines. It's an easy place to hide. Hell," he looked around at the empty table across from them, "if things get too hot, he could jump a shrimp boat and be gone for six or seven weeks at a time."

Kate nodded. "What's the election got to do with it?"

"They've got a senatorial election coming up. One of the candidates may have APF money behind him. He looks like a winner. The locals have someone inside—keeping an eye on things."

Gruber sat upright and took a drink of his mineral water. He frowned like someone drinking Bromo-Seltzer. "I got a friend, Charlie, down there who'll keep us up on it. He owes me a favor."

Kate nodded. Cops seemed to thrive on favors. She wondered what he'd done for the cop in Corpus—covered his ass, faked some evidence, wrung out a confession. "I'll get down to Corpus and have a look around," she said.

"Where you going to look?" Gruber moved his chair closer to hers as if he couldn't hear well.

"Bud always said to hide in plain sight."

She couldn't name the places, but she knew where people worked when they had something to hide—convenience stores, day labor, restaurants, landscaping, anyplace where the work was hard, the pay low, and no one asked questions.

Gruber studied her intently, as if seeing her for the first time. He shifted in his chair, glancing off to one side, then back at her. "Want another?" he said, indicating her half-full glass. Kate shook her head.

He looked off into the distance again, then cleared his throat and leaned forward, resting his elbows on the table. "Can I ask you something?" His voice had taken on a flirtatious quality, and he didn't wait for her answer. "You ever think about switching to men?"

Kate took a swallow of beer, then set the glass down. "No, have you?"

Gruber laughed. "Not since I was twelve." There was a long moment of silence at the table. "Well, I had to ask."

Kate took another sip of beer, and Gruber watched a flower-decorated boat making its way past them along the riverbank.

After they left the bistro, they walked in awkward silence. When Gruber spoke again, he was all business. "We better travel separately, just in case. I'll rent you a car here. You drive, I'll fly. Get yourself settled. I'll be in touch."

"How'll you know where I am?"

"I'll know," Gruber said. He looked off into the distance, like there was something to see, but Kate had the feeling he didn't want to meet her eyes. Damn right he didn't. What the son of a bitch was saying was he'd be watching her.

"Well fuck you, too," Kate said under her breath.

CHAPTER ELEVEN

I-37 between San Antonio and Corpus is a flat ribbon so boring to drive that Kate popped her rental Chevy Corsair into cruise control and thought about crawling into the back to catch a nap. She tried recapturing the impatience she and Dwight had felt when their mother drove this stretch on the way to Corpus in the summertime. They rented a tiny house on Padre Island, where they could spend every day on the beach and eat outside by a clothesline strung with drying swimming suits. On the way down, she and Dwight would count auto license plates, then windmills and, finally, minutes until they saw Corpus shimmering in the distance.

But the Corpus that finally stretched out before her was an aging whore of a city. The air was soft and salty, but refineries dotted the skyline, giving the air the odor of a leaking cookstove. They'd be all lit up at night like a giant carnival, but in the pitiless Gulf sunlight they were an expressionist vision of hell, with their tanks and superstructures topped by gas flares that burned the sky.

Downtown was as vacant as if an air raid warning had sounded, the office buildings staring blankly out at the Gulf and the parking garages standing empty. Toward the edge of town, she found a chain of malls and, beyond that, tracts of houses, first flat ramblers in developments with Spanish names, then later, out toward the Naval Air Station, sprawling rows of faded frame houses lined up along unpaved streets. Here, at the seamy edge of town, carports replaced garages, and the yards were filled with rotting cars and unrecognizable equipment.

Kate tried to remember what little history she'd learned about the area. The town rested at the center of a bay that was sheltered by the barrier of Padre Island. The original inhabitants shunned the malarial interior, preferring the white barrier beaches with their wealth of fish and waterfowl. They'd been extirpated by white settlers and remained only in a few names—Port Aransas, the Aransas Pass Indians high school football team, and a notation her mother had read to her from the *Blue Book of Texas* that the area was once inhabited by cannibalistic Indians. Kate smiled to herself. The winners always get to decide that the losers deserved their fate.

She also remembered her mother's friends: Navy pilots and their beautiful wives, bulky engineers in town to build military bases, and munitions plants. More men than women, if she remembered correctly.

From what she could see, Texas had never recovered from the oil bust of the eighties. The wells had dried up, and every pump jack she passed stood idle. There were so signs of new drilling. If oil was coming in, it had to be from the Middle East. Texas had been sucked dry.

She found rows of generic chain motels that reminded her of some television commercial—she couldn't quite remember which one it was. What she wanted, though, was something small, out of the way, maybe with a table and a kitchenette where she could drink coffee and look out a window. She drove around till she found an area that had once been a popular beachfront and casino. These days a few motels remained, surrounded by shops selling tourist junk and vacant lots bisected by streets overgrown with weeds.

The place called itself the Sandy Shores. She rang the bell at the desk until she roused the owner, a stocky man whose paunch hung over the Walther PK strapped to his belt. He showed her a room facing the bay with a kitchenette looking out at a weed-overrun block of land marked by the concrete steps of vacation cottages that had long since been torn down.

"Nine-inch walls," the owner said. He patted the one nearest him fondly. "It'll stop anything, even a nine-millimeter." Before Kate could ask whether it would need to stop a nine-millimeter, he'd moved on out the door.

The room was painted a pale green that clashed with the orange bedspread. The smell of disinfectant lingered in the air—a reminder of the smell of the intake unit at Lexington. It should have repelled her, but she felt oddly comforted.

She followed him back to the office, registered as Nadine Parker from Wichita Falls and paid a week in advance from her wad of cash. Then she wandered down to the beach. A row of refineries lined the murky ship channel behind her. Up ahead, just offshore, a decommissioned aircraft carrier loomed like a beached leviathan. Someone, probably the Chamber of Commerce, had decided the area needed a tourist attraction so they towed it in and anchored it just off North Beach.

Kate found a spot and sat in the sand, sifting golden grains through her fingers, watching it fly in the breeze. Gulls, both ringbilled and Franklin's, lounged around, resting in small flocks, occasionally approaching her with an officious strut, as if they were about to demand identification. An elderly woman moving with the determination of an athlete marched past, her arms pumping in rhythm with her feet. She had red weights strapped to each wrist, which gave her the appearance of someone flashing messages with each step. Kate started to speak but noticed the woman's ears were plugged with earphones. She wondered what the woman listened to—Led Zeppelin, rap music, inspirational lectures by Sri Chinmoy.

A ship left the channel, engines throbbing. A lone sailor rested on the rail of the bow, looking landward. Kate raised her arm and waved, and he returned the wave, one lone traveler greeting another.

CHAPTER TWELVE

She wasn't sure how he did it because she never spotted him following her, but Gruber knew she was in town. When she returned from the beach, she found a note with a phone number slid under her door. She called from a pay phone outside the motel office. Gruber answered on the first ring and told her to meet him in the morning at the Sutter Wildlife Refuge. "Its right in town," he said, "but it's nice and private. No receivers, no mikes."

"They got mikes that can pick up a fart in a windstorm," Kate said.

"So, maybe I want to show you some birds." And he hung up.

Light was just breaking when she arrived at the refuge and found an empty parking lot surrounded by a few palm trees. Minutes later, Gruber pulled in, driving a bright red Jeep Renegade that was an almost perfect match for his windbreaker.

"Where'd you manage to rent that?" Kate asked.

Gruber's grin said he just knew things. He extracted a backpack from the trunk and motioned for her to follow him down a gravel trail to a boardwalk that cut through a marsh. As they walked, he pointed out ducks feeding in the water.

"Teal" he said, "blue and green-winged."

Kate stopped in her tracks, mesmerized. Gruber stopped, too, but went on naming birds—mallards, redheads, coots. She'd never seen such a variety of waterfowl in one place. It was their colors that surprised her. They were so much more vivid than on the flat pages of her field guide. She fixed on a green-headed duck with a bill made for scooping.

"Shoveler?" she called out, frightening the ducks with the noise of her excitement.

Gruber nodded, surprised.

"Hell, they're not that rare," Kate said.

They followed the boardwalk to an observation platform that looked out on a tidal basin. Even though Corpus had crept around on two sides, and the Navy had claimed the far shore for an air station, birds still came here by the hundreds. Gulls lifted and landed effortlessly, tall white egrets and black-necked stilts curved their fragile necks in the breeze, occasionally lowering their beaks to the mud like stiltwalkers amid the tiny shorebirds that were busily sorting through grains of muddy sand. Here and there, a white pelican lounged on a sandbar like a brooding piece of garden sculpture.

They walked in silence, tasting the air and listening to the wet sounds of birds washing and preening.

"Anybody pick you up here?" Gruber asked after awhile.

"Nobody but you."

They moved softly so they wouldn't disturb the birds. Gruber extracted his binoculars from his backpack and scanned the water.

"My buddy here says he's been having a little moral dilemma about helping me." He put the accent on the first syllable of dilemma.

"But you persuaded him?"

Gruber lowered his glasses and grinned briefly. "I reminded him of the last night at the 1998 Peace Officers Convention in Las Vegas, when he and a certain young lady became very, very close. It served to resolve his dilemma real fast."

"And?"

"And we're having breakfast with him first thing tomorrow at Pepe's down on Chaparral Street. He'll fill us in." Gruber was scanning the shoreline as he talked. "But I can tell you the trail gets real cold real fast. He says the APF is all over the place down here, and they have several people inside but nobody knows whether they're just putting on uniforms and playing soldier or if they're up to something."

"With all the ordnance around here," Kate gestured in the direction of the Naval Air Station, "they gotta be pushing weapons."

Gruber shrugged in reply. Kate frowned and looked off into the distance. If the locals couldn't get a snitch to tell them about weapons shipments, something was wrong. Either the snitch was on the APF's payroll or the locals were in on the trade. She sighed heavily but decided to let it go. "Any word of Bud?" she said.

It was easier somehow if she didn't think of him as her father.

"Not a thing." Gruber said. "If he's around, he's keeping real quiet."

Neither of them spoke for awhile. Gruber scanned the water. Kate watched a grey shorebird with a long ungainly bill as it made its way along the edge of the water, bobbing up and down, searching for food.

She relaxed against the rail, letting the rich salt smell of the marsh wash over her. Gulls made a steady background roar as they lifted off and landed in some pattern known only to themselves.

"Can I borrow those glasses?" she asked suddenly.

Gruber passed his binoculars over, then watched as she focused on a brownish shorebird standing in shallow water and dipping methodically up and down.

"Dowitcher?" he asked.

"Shortbilled." Kate was surprised how certain she was of that. It was as if the bird had popped off the page of the field guide and taken life in front of her.

She scanned the shore until she came to a large bird standing motionless in the water. It was gunmetal grey with a reddish chest, and it stood on one leg, patiently waiting for a fish to pass. "Reddish egret." She was nearly laughing with delight.

"How'd you know that?"

"You sent that stupid book. I memorized it." She handed the glasses back.

"We may not be seeing the old man, but this has got to be the perfect place for him. Over there," Gruber gestured toward the Naval air station, "you got the Navy. In town, they got another helicopter station. Across the bay, they're making mines." He shook his head. "Fact is, you could hijack anything up to weapons grade plutonium around this place. If the old man isn't running something here, I'll turn my badge in."

Well, at least he picked that up, Kate thought to herself. With this much ordnance around, supply sergeants, even an occasional officer passed over for promotion, could be persuaded to trade the odd truck-load of material for a little cash.

Kate took the binoculars again and studied a flock of ducks, admiring the way they moved in and out of the reeds at the water's edge. When Gruber reclaimed them he told her it was time to go.

"Follow me in your car," he said.

He led her to South Padre Island Drive, staying on the service road until he came to a row of dismal stores that looked like they'd been left behind when something better opened up. He stopped in front of one with the ambiguous name RVP Services and a display window full of electronic equipment—cellular phones, wires, grey metal boxes. He was inside the door by the time Kate caught up with him.

"You aren't thinking of getting me a computer?" she said.

Gruber was examining a display of pagers. Kate had heard talk about them, but when she'd gone inside only doctors actually wore them.

"We need some equipment." Gruber spoke with the confidence of a man in his element.

A salesman joined them. His short-sleeved white shirt and tie did nothing to make him look less adolescent

"I'm Ray Gruber." Gruber extended his hand. "I believe you got my e-mail."

"Sure did." The man sounded like his voice might still break. "I've got everything you asked for." He motioned for them to follow him behind the counter to a back room, where he produced a cardboard box from under a counter and opened it.

"The tracking system you wanted wasn't available, but we got this one, which is a little better. It's active for thirty days, and you can track within a hundred mile radius."

Kate said, "Ray," but she was off to one side, where he could pretend not to hear.

Gruber examined the literature briefly, then spread the equipment out in front of him—a small oscillating screen and a lot of cords. "Can I operate this off a battery?"

"You can even plug it into your cigarette lighter."

Gruber was nodding. He and the young salesman were in a techno-nerd communion.

"And this Nokia cell phone you asked for." It looked like something from a *Star Trek* episode.

She picked up the phone. "Can I use this to stun people?"

Gruber frowned, and the salesman looked pained.

"How long to activate it?" Gruber asked.

The salesman smiled with pleasure as they returned to the task. "We have the whole system ready for you."

"Ray." Kate was more insistent. "How about the wire?"

The salesman was as excited as Gruber.

"You asked for the same model the police use. I couldn't get that for you, but I found this one." He pulled out yet another cardboard box. "It's smaller and lighter, and," he paused, "it's made by Sony."

Gruber nodded, impressed.

"Ray." Kate wouldn't be put off this time. "Can we talk a minute?"

"I'll just wait out front. You folks take your time." The salesman stepped gingerly around a display of modems and wireless networks and left them alone.

"What's all this for?"

"These are cell phones." He spoke slowly like she might not understand and opened his jacket to show her his own cellular in a leather belt holster. "We need to be able to find each other fast." He pulled out his own. "You ever use one of these?"

"Christ, no. We were still using field phones when I went in."

"They're cheap, portable, and," he held the phone at arm's length to admire it, "very hard to tap."

Kate frowned. "Didn't Prince Charles in England get tapped using one of those?"

Gruber put the phone back in its box. "You can do it, but you have to have a lot of equipment tuned into just the right channel. And," he gave her a conspiratorial look, "I got me an ol' boy here who can clone this thing for us so nobody'll ever be able to tap it."

Kate decided she didn't want to know how somebody cloned a telephone. "So what am I supposed to do with this?" She gestured to

74

the array of equipment spread out in front of her.

"You're supposed to carry it. I'll get you a holster, unless you'd rather carry a purse." He stopped for a moment, pleased with his own joke.

"And the transmitter?"

"Well, you're going to have to put it somewhere where it can't be seen, someplace," he hesitated, "personal."

Kate folded her arms over her chest and looked up at him. "Like up my ass."

"I wasn't thinking exactly of that."

"And the wire?" Kate was pacing around the room, picking up objects and setting them down abruptly.

"We might need it."

People talked about wearing the wire at Lexington. It was a synonym for informer, the lowest form of life on earth. Kate drew a deep breath. She had signed on to catch her father, not to be a goddamned snitch. She turned away for an instant. She could walk out the door and leave this whole thing behind. And do what? She asked herself. She picked up the phone again, trying to convince herself it wasn't a toy.

Gruber was reading a miniature printed insert that accompanied the tracking device.

"Do we really need all this?"

"We do."

Gruber's jaw took a set she'd never seen before. He was the cop, and he was running her, just like he would any other informer.

CHAPTER THIRTEEN

It wasn't hard to spot Pepe's Cafe. For one thing, it was the only remaining business on the block, but if that wasn't enough, the brilliant pink paint with turquoise trim made it stand out like a carnival prize in a mortuary. A middle-aged Hispanic man came from behind the cash register to greet Kate and show her to a booth nestled against a peach-colored wall that was trying to pass for adobe.

The breakfast crowd was drifting in—youngish women trying to look like someone in the cast of *Friends* ordered coffee for take-out while men wearing ties and white shirts occupied the tables, alone or in pairs, reading their newspapers. Two waitresses, dressed identically in jeans and blue T-shirts, glided around, refilling coffee cups and carrying plates of eggs and plastic bowls of hot tortillas.

Gruber arrived a few minutes later, trailed by a short man with a bushy mustache and a bald head ringed with light brown hair. He had on a J.C. Penney suit that he wore like a man unused to civilian clothes. Kate pictured him first in blue for police then in dun-colored gabardines for sheriff.

Gruber slid in opposite Kate. The man hesitated a moment, checking the room before he followed. When the waitress appeared with coffee and menus, he opened his and ducked behind it as if he could hide from recognition. Gruber opened a menu and buried himself in it, leaving Kate waiting for an introduction. When none came, she extended her hand. "I'm Kate Porter."

Ignoring her hand, the man turned to Gruber, "She doesn't need to know my name."

Gruber looked up. "He's a friend, Kate. He just wanted to see you for himself."

"I'm taking a hell of a chance for you," the bald man said to Gruber, as if by ignoring Kate he could lessen the risk, "even talking to you unofficially and all."

"I know you are." Gruber stopped himself, strangling the syllables that would have been the man's name. "Don't think we're not grateful."

The man nodded, satisfied that his efforts were being acknowledged. When the waitress stopped at the table to take their order, he waved her away. "We're not ready yet," he said as if he were in charge. He watched her back until she was an acceptable distance away, then cleared his throat and began to speak as if someone had posed a question for him.

"I've got a hell of a lot of unidentified bodies here, mostly illegals. But I've run records for the past five years and I could only hit on a couple of likelies." He stopped, squinting, looking at Kate for the first time. "Any possibility of dental records?"

"You said he'd help find Bud," she said to Gruber.

"He might be dead." Gruber sounded apologetic.

Kate shook her head. "He's not dead."

The two men were silent for a moment.

"I just know that," Kate said. She looked at the two men, trying to imagine how she sounded. Pretty dumb was her guess so she changed the subject and answered the bald man's question. "He had all his teeth pulled in Matamoros in '79. He was worried about dental problems if he had to go underground."

"And he was six-foot two, two-hundred ten pounds the last time you saw him?" the man was searching the inside pocket of his jacket. He extracted a pencil and tiny notepad.

Kate nodded and took a sip of her coffee. She tried to remember the last time she'd seen him. He'd put on weight and developed a soft midsection that hung over his belt buckle and he'd dyed his hair black. He'd also grown a scruffy beard that he made scruffier by darkening it to match his hair. His false teeth never fit well, so he seldom wore them, leaving his face to fall slack and his mouth soft with the jaw line making a gentle bend that folded under the flesh of his face.

The bald man shook his head. "The six-footer we found was last year and it says here," he flipped open his notebook, "that he had three of his teeth."

Gruber sighed and shifted in his seat. He opened a cream container and dribbled three drops into his coffee.

"Sorry," the bald man said. He was looking steadily at Kate now, as if expecting her to say something.

Gruber caught Kate's eye. "Well, its just something we had to check."

Kate took a deep breath. She was surprised at how relieved she felt to know her father wasn't dead. But that wasn't what Gruber's friend was saying. What he meant was if Bud was dead, he wasn't dead in Corpus.

Gruber had turned to the bald man, "What have you got on the APF?"

The bald man lowered his voice another notch and leaned closer. "There's two or three guys we've been keeping an eye on, but Jim Morris is the main one. He's got fifty acres upriver and he orders ammonium nitrate like crazy."

"He manufacturing bombs up there?" Gruber asked.

"All he's got up there is mesquite and cactus, so we know he's not fertilizing anything. Lots of trucks go in and out of there, and on weekends you can hear gunfire clear into the next town."

Kate kept quiet, sensing that the bald man wanted to hear nothing from her.

"Could be manufacturing a stockpile." Gruber looked into the distance, trying to put the pieces together in his mind.

"Maybe, but I don't know why you'd bother. If you've got the cash you can buy anything you want here."

"You hear about any thefts?" Gruber asked.

The bald man shook his head. "It wouldn't be outright theft. It'd more than likely be what those military guys call leakage. Some supply officer just slips out a little bit here and there."

Kate looked down at the table, studying her spoon, afraid to look directly at Gruber. If this guy was his best hope then they were sunk. If the APF was in this area at all, they'd be trading weapons. Bud believed he'd practically invented the weapons trade.

Gruber must have sensed a dead end and opened a new line of questioning. "Got any leads on what they're using for cash?"

"We're not sure." The bald man's gaze wavered a second and he frowned slightly.

He's lying, Kate thought and looked at Gruber to see if he'd noticed.

"All we're sure of is that Jim Morris hasn't paid taxes in seven years—says he doesn't believe in it."

"Seven years in arrears and nobody's dropped a warrant on him?" Gruber asked.

"No way." The bald man shook his head slightly. "Nobody wants to go in there and get shot up for chump change for the county. Sheriff says it's not worth it." He gave the kind of lame smile people give when they say you can't fight city hall.

Gruber leaned back slightly, stretching himself in his chair. "So how could I meet this ol' boy?" He was already starting to sound Texas.

"You can't. He never leaves the property. But his wives do—all three of them."

Gruber raised his eyebrows.

"Claims it's in the Bible." The bald man was smiling now and Kate sensed that the men would have had a different conversation if she hadn't been there.

"They must have left that part out when I was singing in the choir at the First Baptist Church." Gruber looked at Kate and grinned.

"He's got a brother-in-law named Bobby Sanford," the bald man said. "He's got a big mouth and he likes free beer. You can find him at the Raceway Bar on weeknights."

"Maybe I'll drop in and buy him a beer and tell him how smart he is."

"What about her?" The bald man nodded toward Kate. "What's she going to do?"

"She's here for back-up. She's going to lay low, aren't you?" Gruber gave her a little nod of encouragement.

Kate smiled, as if in total agreement.

Gruber leaned in closer to the bald man. "We're going to need you to keep a close check on your man in the APF. If anything's coming down, I want to know it fast."

The man pushed himself away from the table slightly, shaking his head. "We got fibbies and Alcohol, Tobacco and Firearms guys all over us, Ray. My boss wants us to keep this whole thing in-house. You let this out and I'm in deep shit, Arkansas."

"Charlie, if this pans out you're going to look like one hell of a peace officer. This guy's been on the lam for fourteen years and you'll be the man on the scene who took him. You could blow this whole thing wide open. Get yourself on *Sixty Minutes*."

Neither man seemed to notice that Gruber had addressed the bald man by name. "It might look real good when your sheriff retires."

The bald man frowned again, calculating the odds, measuring the risks. "I do this and we're even," he said at last, watching Gruber warily.

"You got it buddy." Gruber was grinning now, satisfied with his deal.

Charlie slid out of the booth and left abruptly, without shaking hands or saying goodbye. He hurried out to the street, stopping once to look around.

Kate looked down at her coffee, which suddenly seemed black and unfriendly. She emptied two creamers in to cheer it up.

The waitress appeared to take their order. Gruber asked for oat-meal with skim milk on the side. Kate ordered a taquito with chorizo sausage and scrambled eggs.

"That stuff'll kill you," Gruber said.

"So?"

Their food arrived. Gruber looked dubiously at his glass of milk. "Are you sure this is skim?" he asked the waitress.

"It's two percent, sir, we don't serve skim."

Gruber poured the milk on his cereal and looked pained, as if he could see the grams of fat jumping from the glass to his midsection, but he dug into his oatmeal as Kate took a bite of taquito. The chorizo was greasy and spicy and eating it reminded her how far she was from the cold rubbery eggs she'd been eating for the last twelve years.

After a couple of bites she stopped, resting her fork on the edge of the plate. "Ray, you think that guy," she motioned with her fork to follow Charlie's exit, "is for real?"

"I hope to Christ he is because we're dead in the water without him."

"But you know damn well that if Bud's here he's running guns."

"And your point is?" Gruber looked restless and impatient.

"The locals don't know shit about this operation. You get in there and you're running straight into people who will just love getting their hands on you."

Gruber glanced down at his watch and started to reach for the check.

Kate reached to restrain him. "They're going to be watching for undercover people."

"I've done undercover before, Kate. I know what I'm doing."

"Okay," was what she said. It was just the opposite of what she thought.

CHAPTER FOURTEEN

In three days, Kate had seen all the malls, eaten lots of fast food and had her fill of sleeping late. She woke just before dawn, too edgy to sleep, and walked three miles to the boat basin, where she dangled her legs off a dock and watched sailboats rock in their berths.

Her mind drifted back to her childhood summers in Port Aransas. Kate remembered hearing that Bud used to come with them, but that must have been when she was a baby, because her only memory was of the three of them—Mama, herself, and Dwight—making the long drive from Amarillo to the Gulf. They usually left at dusk, which Mama said was to avoid the heat, but Kate thought she must have liked driving in the dark, over deserted highways, with her children sleeping in the back seat. She remembered waking at strange gas stations and listening to pump boys flirting with Mama as they filled the tank.

They spent every day at the beach. Toward evening a local girl named Luz appeared and made supper while Mama showered and retired behind her curtain to dress. Kate always sat cross-legged on one end of the bed while her mother perched on the other, peering into the mirror of her makeup case while she applied eyeshadow, foundation, and other mysterious ointments that transformed her into a magical creature smelling of powder and Chanel No. 22.

During their last summer, a man they were told to call Uncle Ted showed up just as they were being put to bed. He was dark, with a gambler's moustache and drove a maroon Cadillac. At first Dwight and Kate didn't like him, but he called them both cowboy and pretend to lose fast-draw contests, staggering back against the wall and saying,

"You got me podner," as Kate and Dwight shot him with their finger pistols.

Uncle Ted had shown up at their home in Amarillo. Kate woke in the night to hear the heavy sound of the Cadillac's door shutting in front of their house. She knew when he phoned because her mother's voice got soft and low, and the calls were short. She was with him that last night, when the Santa Fe freight struck the Cadillac at a crossing halfway between Amarillo and White Deer.

Kate pulled herself back to the present and wandered around until she found a fancy coffee shop whose shelves were filled with over-priced chrome coffee machines and stark, modern cups. She ordered a cappuccino and tried to look like it wasn't her first cup ever while she sat at a round plastic table, leafing through a discarded *Houston Chronicle*. Then she noticed a map of Corpus Christi Bay on the wall. Throwing the paper to one side, she rose and stood in front of it, tracing the route to Port Aransas with her index finger.

Why not? she asked herself. No one cared what she did anyway. It wasn't like she had to be anywhere. For the first time in twelve years, she could go anywhere she pleased.

So she drove to Port Aransas. Once across the thin, sandy Packery Channel, she was on the barrier reef that divided Corpus Christi Bay from the inland lagoon called the Laguna Madre. Barrier dunes blocked her view of the Gulf, and the island itself was a forbidding spit of sand broken only by clumps of sea grass and cactus. Some of her childhood excitement returned. This was the stretch of the trip where she and Dwight would begin to count phone poles, guessing how many they had left until they got to the beach.

The Lone Star Lodge was gone—destroyed by a storm or bull-dozed in the name of progress—and replaced by a restaurant called the Dolphin Cove, which billed itself as seafood heaven. Kate stood by her car, looking around for something familiar. The street, which had once been lined with nests of tourist cottages and small motels, was now filled with RV lots. Beyond, condominiums loomed, poised like megaliths. She felt her chest tighten like she wanted to cry. She clenched her fists so tightly that her nails dug into her palms, and the tears retreated until nothing was left but a heavy feeling in her chest. There was nothing left to cry over, she told herself; it was all gone, and that was just as well.

From inside her jacket pocket, the cellular phone buzzed impatiently. She fumbled around with it, pushing buttons until she found the one marked Connect. Gruber wanted to meet up with her. He gave directions to a place called Fish Pass. It wasn't far—in fact she'd crossed a bridge called Fish Pass on the way to Port Aransas.

"Half an hour," he said.

Fish Pass was the sandy river slicing through Padre Island from the Gulf to the Laguna Madre. As she pulled up beside Gruber's Jeep, she could see a thin stream of water where dowitchers and willets teetered on spindly legs using their needle-like bills to sort each grain of sand in a relentless search for food. A film of high clouds had moved in from the north, weakening the sunshine and washing out the landscape to a dull grey.

Gruber was nowhere in sight, so she parked and squatted in the sand, watching the inevitable gulls floating in to rest on a sandbar. Gruber soon emerged from under the concrete bridge spanning the pass. An offshore wind ruffled his hair, making him look younger and happier than she'd ever seen him.

"I got to first base," he said.

"Tell me about it."

Gruber hunkered beside her. He began to sift sand, as if the act would stir his memory.

"Well, I spent the last three nights drinking in too many bars till I found me some good ol' boys."

Kate knew the type—big men, dressed in combat fatigue pants and T-shirts with slogans like "Kill 'em all, let God sort 'em out."

"I didn't find the brother-in-law, but I did get me a nibble. I met a fellow called Billie Jack. Actually," Gruber looked sheepish, "everyone else called him Willie. He took me around to three or four bars, even to a gentleman's club. I damn near had to pull him off some dancer's tits. Thought he was going to have a heart attack."

Gruber laughed at the memory. "Anyway, we ended up at his house with his mama making breakfast at three A.M. He starts telling me about something called the Organization."

"Is that what he called it?"

Gruber nodded. "Said they have regular encampments, weapons training, and some other things that he couldn't talk about."

"What you tell him about yourself?"

Gruber smiled. "I got a good story. I just got out of the Missouri Penitentiary after a stretch for grand theft, auto. I got connected with Aryan Nation inside, and I mean to stay connected now I'm out."

"And he bought that?"

Gruber nodded. "He gave me a copy of your old man's book. Told me to read it and come to an encampment if I wanted. Said he'd show me around."

Gruber looked proud of himself. "So, what do you think?"

"I think you met a geek with a big mouth." Kate watched the wind make little ripples in the water.

"He's taking me to meet some people." Gruber sounded irritated, as if she were missing the point.

"Ray, if he bought you as Aryan Nation then he's too dumb to be anything more than a wanna-be." She looked up at him. Even on a bad day, Gruber was too straight-arrow to pass for the tattooed, shaven-headed thugs who proclaimed themselves Aryan Nationalists. "I'm telling you, it doesn't mean a damn thing. The real APF doesn't call itself the Organization, and they don't let guys like Willie at anything more than a public meeting. They're ready for people like you. Its called infiltration." She pronounced the syllables separately. "And they teach workshops on it."

Gruber looked down at the sand, frowning, searching for words. "I think I can use this man. I've worked informants before." He raised his eyes to look at her. His voice was level, and he seemed to be trying hard to keep himself from lashing out at her.

Kate sighed heavily, then stopped to follow the shadow of a gull as it skimmed across the sand. "Has anyone been following you?" she asked.

Gruber shook his head.

Kate scraped the sand with her finger. "Me neither. Something's funny. The APF picked me up in Amarillo and tailed me all the way to Waco. I shook them." Gruber was listening, frowning, "But they should be turning the whole state upside down looking for me."

Gruber's forehead wrinkled.

"We aren't really undercover," Kate said, "so where are they? Why aren't we seeing anybody?"

Gruber twisted his head to one side. "Maybe they haven't got here yet?" His voice rose in a question.

Kate shook her head. "Maybe we've been made. Bud knows where we are. Now he's laying back, waiting to see what we'll do."

As if on cue, they both stood and looked at the horizon. Then they looked away. Neither had wanted to be the first to check to see if someone seemed to be looking in their direction.

At length, Kate spoke. "Why don't I scratch around town some more, Ray, see what I can turn up. It'll give me something to do."

"You think you can do better than me?" Gruber said.

Kate stood up, "In my sleep."

"Just be real careful," Gruber said, sounding like he wanted her to know who was in charge of things.

CHAPTER FIFTEEN

Downtown Corpus reminded her of one of those post-apocalypse movies where all the people are dead, and the cities stand empty. You could shoot an arrow down main street and not hit a living thing. There was nothing but rotting buildings, empty foundations and the hulks of abandoned hotels.

She parked near the ruins of the old courthouse and walked around until she found its replacement—all pink stone and mauve trim. It loomed over a street filled with used furniture stores and billboards advertising bail bondsmen. This was the first time she'd seen people out on the streets—lounging, waiting for a bus, standing outside pawnshops or sitting on benches waiting for the check, the letter, the phone call that would save their lives.

She was close to the shadow world that she knew existed half a step beneath the surface, where people went by first names or handles like Smokey or Nevada, where if you worked, you got paid by the day, and you kept your eye on the front door so that if anyone who looked like the heat appeared you could slide out the back.

She began with John's Ribs 'N' Tacos. She took a stool at the counter, ordered coffee and turned herself halfway around to survey the customers. Several groups of Hispanic men talked quietly. Their faces had the lean and haunted look of men who labored hard for a pay envelope that was empty by Saturday morning. Towards the rear, she spotted a thin, heavily bearded Anglo, skin dark with dirt, wearing everything he owned. There were several women around, some with small children, but most of them alone. At a table in the front sat a large woman with hair that looked as if she'd bleached it at home. Her hands rested on her rolls of fat, and her blank face said she expected nothing at all.

Kate leaned back, trying to catch someone's eye, so she could smile, nod, make some kind of contact. But no one responded.

She moved on to Super Taco. The place was nearly empty except for a lank-haired waitress who looked like she'd been there since the day it opened. Kate tried to get her talking by asking how business was, but the woman just nodded, filled Kate's coffee cup and vanished into the kitchen.

At Pete's Super Grill, she tried to strike up a conversation with a grizzled man on the seat next to her but got nothing more than an empty stare and a blast of morning winebreath.

By the time she reached the Town Talk Cafe, she had a sour stomach and a headache. She stopped outside to buy a paper. Maybe it would give her something to talk about.

Inside, she ordered a glass of milk. After a few minutes, a youngish man entered. His face had the sharp creases of someone who didn't eat regularly, and his long hair hung in lank, dirty strands. He paused at the door for a minute, then took the stool next to Kate and studied the menu. When the waitress approached, he closed it decisively and said, "I'll just have coffee." He sat quietly for a moment.

"You mind if I look at some of that paper?" he asked Kate.

She handed him the second section of the *Caller-Times*. When his coffee arrived, he poured in three creams.

Kate signaled the waitress. "I'd like the two eggs over easy, a side of steak and biscuits." She caught the man's eye as he looked up from the paper. "I'm real hungry this morning," she said.

The man smiled in agreement. "I know what you mean."

"Care to join me?" Kate pointed at the place in front of her where her plate of food would rest. The man looked blank, but when he got what she was asking his grin widened and he nodded.

"Just to keep you company."

Kate signaled the waitress and pointed at the man, asking for a second order.

"You on the road long?" She had on her best Texas bar girl voice.

"Too long."

"Where you from?"

"Tulsa," he said, "but I can't get no work there. I heard about a job in Lubbock, but by the time I got there the fella'd closed up, so I hitched to Dallas and worked planting trees all summer."

The waitress arrived with their food. Kate pushed her eggs from one side of the plate to the other while the man dug into his.

"Been down here long?" she asked.

The man wiped his mouth with the back of his hand and swallowed before answering. "I heard there was work here in the building trades, but I ain't worked more than two days in a month." He buttered a biscuit and took a bite. "I'm going out to Aransas Pass today, see if I can get on with a shrimp boat."

Kate nodded as if she knew all about shrimp boats. "I'm here looking for my daddy," she said.

The man stopped eating and looked over at her.

Kate drew a deep breath, as if what she were about to say was difficult. "He's been on the road a long time. I just thought I might be able to help him out if I could find him. You know where fellas might hang out?"

The man started to shake his head, but before he could start the motion Kate reached out and touched his arm. "It'd mean a lot to me and my mama to see him again."

The man finished his breakfast and shoved his plate to one side, resting both elbows on the counter and thinking.

"I could even pay a little," Kate said softly.

His eyes flicked in agreement. She pulled a twenty from her jacket pocket, folded it and covered it with her palm to slide it in front of him. He took the money quietly. It was enough to pay for a pint and a shower. There'd be no trips to Aransas Pass today.

"You might try the library. Some of them old guys hang there every day. At least till the guards chase them off." He chewed loudly, then looked at her out of the corner of his eyes. "You ain't the cops are you?"

"Do I look like a cop?"

The man shook his head. "You can't always tell these days."

Kate gave him a smile as she stood up and laid down a dollar bill for the tip. When she looked back from the cash register, the dollar was gone, so she left another for the cashier to give the waitress.

The library was built of the same pink and mauve stone as the courthouse—the city must have gotten a bargain on the stuff—and it faced rows of empty streets lined with palms and the foundations of vanished houses. A small park lay behind, filled with live oak and renata trees and the Gulf's scorching heat and salt. Even though it was November and the trees were bare, the grass beneath them was green.

Kate parked in the lot beside the library and watched the steady stream of people who entered and left—matrons with small children, men in business suits, winter Texans in their pastel running suits, solitary men, thin and bearded, who seemed to be coming from the little park.

The lone men were the ones who interested her. On the door of the library a sign announced, "NO BACKPACKS OR BEDROLLS ALLOWED!" So you had to risk your pack if you were going to spend a day in the Corpus library.

What she wanted was the reading room, because that's where people with too much time could burrow into a newspaper and catch a nap. A circulation clerk directed her toward the rear of the building, where she found a collection of circular tables edged by racks of newspapers hung on wooden rods. Seated at the tables and surrounding armchairs were the solitary men, papers open so it looked like they were reading. That way the guard wouldn't catch them with their heads on the table and throw them out.

Off to one side, at a desk marked TECHNOLOGY, an apple-shaped woman with a pom-pom of silvery blue hair sat talking on the phone. Her voice boomed over the shuffle of footsteps and turning pages as she made successive phone calls inquiring about Donald's ulcer, Marie's cold and Ina's arthritis. In between calls, she kept a cold eye on the men in the reading room. Off to one side of her desk, a handful of people stood in line like supplicants waiting for a blessing until she took a break to direct them to the books they asked for.

The library at Lexington had been a silent, book-filled room run by an inmate named Helen, who had been the librarian as long as anyone could remember. Hers were the only rules in Lexington that could

never be bent. No spitting, no talking, no defacing of reading material, and every book—she pronounced every syllable of this separately,
for emphasis, when new inmates arrived—was to be returned to her
desk on penalty of banishment. And once Helen said you were out,
you were out. Old Helen would have had a stroke if people had talked
and shuffled around the way they did here.

Just before eleven-thirty, a pale young woman arrived to take the
apple-shaped woman's place. Kate followed in the older woman's
wake to the hallway.

"I wonder if I might have a word?" Kate talked as loud as the
woman had over the phone, which made her turn and look at Kate as
if she'd cursed in a church.

"You're here every day, aren't you?"

"Except weekends." The woman's tone of voice said there was
some significance to this.

"I'm looking for a man who comes here a lot. Maybe you could
help me."

Kate tried to make her smile pleasant, but the woman looked at
Kate narrowly before she answered. "I never pay any attention to the
periodical section." She turned away.

"I didn't say the periodical room." Kate called after her, but the
woman moved on with the determination of a barge going upstream.

Kate turned back to find a young black guard standing at the edge
of the periodical room. She modified her story slightly. "I'm trying to
find him to pay him the money I owe him. It's real important to me."

She gave him a rough description of her father. The guard bent
down, allowing her to speak into his ear, and he looked at the floor,
nodding at her words. When she got to the blue eyes, he looked up.

"There was one old guy. He was a regular till just lately. Comes
in, gets books on wars and stuff like that. He sits up real straight and
sharp like he was a soldier or something."

"Anything else?"

The guard thought for a minute, then he smiled like Kate had said
something funny. "There is one thing. He looks me up and down like
he's checking my uniform. Damn if he don't remind me of my drill
sergeant."

"Any idea where they go when they leave here?"

The guard shook his head.

"Into the nearest wine bottle."

She was just getting into her car when the cell phone sounded with the insistent buzz of an angry insect. She fumbled in her jacket pocket until she got her hand around it, then started pushing buttons. She'd get this sucker right yet.

It was Gruber. He'd been at the Corpus cop, Charlie's, office reading files all morning. When she told him where she was, he promised to meet her in five minutes.

Gruber arrived on foot, and they walked into the park behind the library. He looked like he'd put in a hard night.

"What's the big deal?" Kate asked. "Your pal Willie been taking you out again?"

Gruber ignored her. "It looks like somebody's got themselves a real business trading stolen weapons and materiel," he said. "The state patrol's stopped a semi heading north. The driver got scared and gave up four other fellas that were supposed to be driving rigs behind him. The patrol's waiting for them now."

"What were they carrying?"

"Crates of M-16A's and Browning .50 caliber. Lots of ammo, too."

Kate nodded and looked into the distance where a scrawny orange tomcat stalked a bird that was pecking at the dust beneath a live oak. This was just the kind of equipment Bud would love to trade.

"Anything besides guns?"

"Not sure. They hadn't finished the search. I'm going to head out to the Naval Air Station and talk to some fella who's the head of security. Then maybe I'll go on over to Ingleside."

"What's over there?"

"The world's biggest land mine factory. I'm wondering if they might be having a little leakage of their own over there."

Gruber promised to phone her later, and Kate stayed behind to watch the sun filtering through the twisted branches of the live oak. A tiny grey bird danced from limb to limb. She squinted to get a better look but it took flight before she could spot any distinguishing features.

The drivers of those semis would roll over, but she didn't figure they would know Bud. He'd get someone else to deal with the help so he could handle the bargaining. There had to be middlemen. They might be more interesting. Maybe, she decided, this would be a good time to shop around for some guns. You never could tell who you'd turn up.

CHAPTER SIXTEEN

First she drove around town looking for gun shops. When she came up blank, she stopped in a coffee shop. Sitting in her booth, staring into what felt like her twentieth cup of coffee for the day, she noticed a Yellow Pages directory hanging from a peg next to the cash register. She took it without asking, looked under G—as in gun—and wrote down several addresses.

The first one she tried was called Bill's Bait and Sports, which turned out to be a dingy shop on a strip mall tucked into one side of South Padre Island Drive. The sign on the roof was faded and peeling, and the windows and door were covered with heavy steel mesh.

The shop was dimly lit and smelled of grease, dust and fish. A minnow tank bubbled in one corner. Unopened boxes were scattered all over the floor, Jumbled boxes of ammunition, webbed belts, surplus backpacks and shoulder bags spilled off the shelves. She paused by a pile of musette bags, some bearing the insignia of the Israeli army, some of the now-defunct German Democratic Republic.

The lone clerk leaned on his counter at the back of the store, talking to a customer. He was a short man whose pasty face got a moldy look from the fluorescent light above his head.

The customer looked as if he'd just come from the kind of job that started at four A.M. and kept on until the whistle blew. His face was burned dark from the sun, and his clothes were caked with grease and oil.

His voice echoed through the store. "Any man that can shoot straight got no need for an assault rifle. You give me a 30-06 and a good scope, and I can stop anything and anybody."

The clerk nodded wisely.

Kate waited. She'd learned years ago that women weren't really welcome in gun stores. The customer droned on about packing his own load, and the price of powder. Finally, he slowed down, and the clerk glanced in her direction.

"I'm looking for a good quality 9 millimeter." Kate smiled, doing her best to look a little confused.

"We don't have any handguns in stock, but we can order it for you. We don't even carry displays."

"Is that the law?"

The clerk and the customer exchanged grins.

"The law of supply and demand. We try to keep some on hand, but they buy us out as soon as we get them in."

Kate said she needed something more immediately, and he directed her to Miller's Gun Shop in the Padre-Staples Mall.

She was unlocking her car when a rusted red pickup down the way caught her eye. She moved closer to have a look. It was on the rear window—a decal: the crossed musket and M-16 of the APF. Okay, she told herself as she pulled out, they're here. You expected that. Stay cool—think of all the things you say to yourself when you are scared.

The Miller shop snuggled just inside the mall, fitting itself neatly beside stores selling toys, health food and running shoes. The showcases gleamed, and the displays were tasteful. Except for the nature of the goods, it could have been a home appliance store. Someone had placed a sign in the window urging people to VOTE ANDERSON NOW—BEFORE IT'S TOO LATE.

The clerk was an older man with a drooping waistline and the tired voice of someone who has seen too much of life. He showed Kate a Glock 9 millimeter and a Browning Hi-Power, in both a matte and polished finish.

"What will I need to do to buy one?" she asked.

"You'll need to fill out this federal form."

He slid a yellow paper at her, and Kate scanned it. Question number three asked whether she was a convicted felon. "And I'll need to see a Texas driver's license."

"And if I don't have one?"

"Then I can't sell you a handgun." His voice was firm but regretful.

She turned on her most helpless smile. "Do you know anyone who could help me out—maybe an independent dealer?"

"I wouldn't know anything about anyone like that." He'd been asked that question hundreds of times before and had given the same answer each time.

Kate started for the door, then turned back. "Do you know about any gun shows?"

He sagged with exhaustion.

"We have a gun show here every day."

Back in the parking lot, she spotted the rusty red pick-up in the row opposite hers. She couldn't see the decal on the rear window, but it sure looked like the truck parked at Bill's Bait and Sports. The driver must have followed her. She gave herself a mental kick in the butt for failing to spot him.

She made a show of searching her pockets, then turned back as if she'd forgotten something. Inside the mall, she wandered from store to store, pausing often to look at the reflections in mirrors and windows, checking for anyone who was paying particular attention to her. On the second floor food court, she ordered a cup of coffee and a greasy croissant and sat at a table blowing on her coffee and scanning for a dark man in greasy work clothes. She didn't find him, and when the coffee and croissant were gone, she began a tour of the second floor shops.

She was checking out the rubber plant outside a fancy clothing store when a flash of color caught her eye—a woman with hair the color of spun copper. And there was something familiar in her walk, in the tilt of her shoulders. The woman wore an expensive-looking white pantsuit, and her hair was pulled back off her face and bound with a wide black ribbon. She was moving away. Without meaning to, Kate roused herself and followed, feeling she couldn't stop but afraid to get too close.

The woman didn't so much walk as stride, just the way Lissa had. Kate followed her through the cosmetics, where she stopped to chat with a clerk, then on to the shoe department, where two salesmen jumped up to greet her. Kate paused next to a set of mannequins posed as if they were in a business conference. The red-haired woman held up a wispy little sandal of a shoe. Her face was in profile. Kate noted that her nose was straight, jutting directly out of her forehead with no inward curve. Just like Lissa's.

Kate's stomach fluttered between weakness and anticipation, and, for a second, she felt as if everyone in the store was about to turn and point at her. The woman looked exactly like Lissa. It was uncanny.

A voice from behind made her turn. "May I help you?"

"No—I..." Kate stammered. "I'm just looking. Thanks."

When she looked again, the woman was gone. With the possibility of someone from the APF following her, she couldn't search the whole store, so she settled for waiting outside. She settled on a bench where she could see both store exits and stared into the store until the security guard became a little too interested.

She had to have been wrong, anyway. The woman she'd known at Lexington, Melissa McEvoy, had been out for four years and was probably well into her third marriage if she hadn't died of a drug overdose. She might even be back in jail, but she sure as hell wasn't in Corpus. Besides, she'd always said she'd get a nose job if she ever got any money.

By the time Kate reached the parking lot, the red pickup was gone. If the owner had been following her, he must have gotten tired and left. She still couldn't push the memory of Lissa out of her head. Ever since she'd gotten out, little things—the scent of lemon, the soft touch of a pillow, a waitress's smile—kept pulling up images of Lissa. And here she was standing in a fucking parking lot in Corpus fucking Christi, Texas, feeling like all the air in her lungs was leaking out through a hole in her chest.

CHAPTER SEVENTEEN

Since gun shops were no help, Kate tried pawnshops. Corpus was full of them, some even advertising with the kind of huge neon signs that marked gas stations on the interstates. She hit four in a row and found them full of televisions, VCRs, even a red wagon or two, but the only weapons for sale were rusting shotguns, the occasional rifle, a handful of aging six-shooters along with one or two tiny .25 caliber whores' pistols with nickel-plated barrels and tiny pink grips.

The last store she visited sat underneath a billboard advertising pawns and bail bonds. The only weapons they had for sale were three monstrous, toothed hunting knives. But there was a Xeroxed sign taped to the inside of the window advertising a gun show at Rockport, some thirty miles up the coast.

She drove out over the Portland Bridge, past tidal pools where white pelicans swam in circles to round up and trap fish, on past silent strings of pump jacks, then through mesquite rangeland to Rockport.

The town was a shrimping port that had transformed itself into a retirement community. Live oak groves sheltered temporary trailers and RVs with northern license plates. Closer to the water, condominium communities perched on the shoreline, waiting for the next hurricane to reduce them to splinters.

Kate followed a series of hand-lettered cardboard signs to the Legion Hall at the edge of town and paid her three dollar admission fee to a woman seated at a table with a sign announcing NO PRESS PERMITTED.

The inside looked like a flea market, with merchandise laid out on folding tables, except that the goods for sale were rifles and handguns instead of knicknacks. The shoppers and sellers were mostly middle-aged men wearing baseball caps and belts with big silver buckles.

She stopped to look at a Russian Makarov pistol. When she'd gone inside, the only Russian weapons were a few AK-47s that came by way of Vietnam or the Middle East. She shook her head at the sight of a Chinese-made AK-47 with a graceful curve in its honey-colored stock. It was beautiful, but when she raised it to aim at a spot on the ceiling it felt too light to be reliable.

She moved on until she found a table of handguns. She picked up a Glock 9 millimeter pistol, handling it, aiming at a spot on the floor. Same problem—too light. She knew cops loved them, but a plastic gun just seemed wrong to her. The dealer caught her eye, though. He was younger that most of the men behind tables, and his curly hair had the groomed look that came from being styled instead of cut.

"That's a Glock 9 millimeter." He gave her the head-on, full-blast smile as if to say he was just the man to teach her what she needed to know. "Are you interested in something for self-defense?"

"Actually, I was looking for something with a little more power." Kate picked up a Smith & Wesson .45 caliber and flipped open the cartridge cylinder. "Like maybe a Cobray." She looked back now, smiling. The Cobray was a scion of the Ingram Mac 10 family, an ugly little box of metal that was sold as a semi-automatic but could be modified to make it spit out thirty-two rounds in less than two seconds. It was a mean little piece, at least until it jammed.

"I don't have any in stock right now. I could show you a .38 caliber detective special here. We recommend these for women."

Kate took the gun he offered. The grip felt light and cheap, like if she fired it, it would rub at the skin connecting her thumb and her palm. It had the feel of a Saturday night special. She set it down.

"I'm also in the market for an M-16 A-2 rifle. Could you maybe help me with that?"

"I don't carry those." The dealer was looking around the room for other customers.

"But you know who does, right?" Kate was leaning in now.

"Sorry." His face closed like a trap door.

Kate drifted on, looking briefly at a Savage rifle—a .22 caliber bolt action, the kind she'd first learned to shoot when she was a little girl. She smiled at the memory of herself roaming the canyon country searching for varmints.

Leaving the Legion hall, she caught sight of two men standing by the open gate of a pickup. The younger one had a baby face, which he tried to disguise with a heavy moustache. His movements were quick, and he was nervous. He was showing a Colt Sportster to an older man, who was holding the weapon at arm's length, examining it critically.

Kate edged close enough to draw an anxious glance from the younger man. The older man said, "I'll think it over and get back to you," and handed back the weapon.

Kate gave the younger man her best smile.

"Maybe you can help me."

The man relaxed a little and drew himself up to take on the look of someone who was in charge of the situation.

"I'm looking for some protection, not those antiques they have in there." She motioned back to the Legion Hall. She had his attention. "I'm looking for a good nine millimeter. No cheap Chinese rip-offs, you understand?"

The man nodded as he reached into the bed of his pickup. He extracted a dark-blue box and flipped it open to reveal a Walther PK.

"I'll give you three hundred fifty dollars," Kate looked at him sideways, "if you can give immediate delivery and no tax."

"No tax here," the man said, shaking his head for emphasis. "No tax ever."

"No federal forms?"

"No forms."

Kate extracted folded bills from her left pocket. He watched as she counted out four of them.

"I need some other, more specialized guns. Maybe you could help me."

The man waited.

"I'm interested in wholesale lots. You handle anything that big?"

He looked nervous, biting his lower lip. "That's more than I can handle." His voice rose. He was afraid of a setup.

Kate extended the money to him. "Maybe you know someone who can?"

The man paused a moment, looking at her hand, then took the bills.

"You want to talk to Joe Ray Thompson."

"And where do I find him?"

"Go to Sam's Place—you know where that is?"

Kate shook her head.

"It's under the JFK Bridge."

"How will I know Joe Ray?"

"Ask Frankie, the bartender, he'll point him out to you."

CHAPTER EIGHTEEN

Kate pulled her suitcase out from behind the pile of dirty clothes and put it on the motel's orange bedspread. She was the proud owner of one wig, a pair of black shoes, a cheap handbag, two pairs of pantyhose and one dress, the dowdy blue number she'd picked up in Amarillo.

Looking at herself in the mirror over the bureau, she saw a lean, windblown woman with lank brown hair and tired eyes. Her jeans were faded to a color just short of fashionable, and there was a pale brown spot in the middle of her shirt where she must have spilled coffee. She dabbed at it with a moistened towel but the spot refused to fade. It was time for a new incarnation. She grabbed her jacket and set out for Padre-Staples Mall.

She strolled from shop to shop until she found a rack of tailored silk blouses—pale blue, rose, navy. She usually liked brighter colors, but these caught her imagination. She touched the fabric, then raised a sleeve to brush her cheek, and she caught herself thinking of Lissa's skin. She dropped the sleeve as if it would burn her. Lissa was coming to mind too often.

She hooked a pale blue and a rose over one finger and let the saleswoman point her to a fitting room, where she stripped off her workshirt and slipped the rose silk over her head. It glided on as softly as a kiss. It had been a long time since anything had touched her so gently. She bought both, and the navy as well.

Farther down the mall, she found racks of Wrangler jeans. She usually wore an eight, but she wanted to show off her butt tonight, so she squeezed herself into a size six and promised to eat nothing more substantial than an orange peel.

She was beginning to get a sense of the look she wanted—somewhere on the expensive side of tough and gaudy. This took her to a leather store where she found the perfect jacket—a black kid western version of a motorcycle jacket lined with satin. The traditional slanted zippers on the upper chest had been replaced with silver buckles engraved with Indian designs. Buckles also held the shoulder epaulets in place and fastened the jacket at the belt line.

Kate was admiring herself in the full-length mirror when the saleswoman appeared, dressed in leather jeans and a western shirt with silver trim. Her hair was flashy and short.

"It's six hundred," the saleswoman said, as if she hated to interrupt a daydream.

"I'll take it."

Kate reached for the roll in her pocket. It was diminishing quickly. At this rate, she'd be lucky to have bus fare by the time they caught up with Bud, if they ever did.

"Where can I get the best haircut in town?" she asked while the woman wrote up the purchase. The woman looked up from her work and regarded Kate thoughtfully.

"Try the Flamante Rose on Staples. Ask for Emilio. Tell him Evelyn sent you."

When Kate telephoned the Flamante Rose, the receptionist said Emilio was busy all day but she'd try working Kate in on Friday.

"Tell him I'll pay fifty dollars extra if he can see me today."

The receptionist put her on hold, returning in a moment to say, "He'll work you in at two, but be on time, okay?"

Kate was five minutes early. The receptionist turned her over to a pink-smocked attendant, who asked if she'd like a changing room. Kate hesitated, confused.

"You know, for your blouse," the attendant said helpfully. Kate looked down at her shirt, shook her head. It was nothing to protect.

She was given a copy of *Elle* magazine and left to wait forty-five minutes until another attendant summoned her to the inner sanctum. Emilio was a stocky man of indeterminate age with dark hair modeled

103

in nouveau Elvis waves. He waited off to one side while the attendant seated and smocked Kate. Then he moved in, studying Kate with the attention of a sculptor examining a piece of raw marble.

"What I need is a makeover," Kate said.

Emilio nodded in agreement.

"I want some makeup and a haircut to die for. Can you do it?"

Emilio moved forward, picking up a strand of her hair, rubbing it between two fingers, examining it critically.

"Have you been cutting this yourself?"

Kate nodded, not wanting to tell him that her cellmate was responsible for the butchery and that for the past twelve years no one had much cared.

He studied it a moment more then nodded resolutely. "I think we can fix it for you." He winked at her image in the mirror, a moment of silent communication between a gay man and a lesbian. "When is it for?"

"Tonight." Kate's voice grew smaller.

"Show me what you'll wear."

The attendant rushed to the waiting area and returned with Kate's packages. She opened them and laid out the contents.

Emilio frowned again.

"Wear the rose with the jacket. It'll soften it." The attendant rustled softly. "Also, get some gold—couple of long gold chains." The attendant gathered up the clothing and disappeared.

He returned to her hair.

"Let's put a rinse on this, bring out the highlights." He seemed to be speculating.

"You mean dye it?"

"Not really dye. We just want to darken it."

Kate's natural color was light brown, darkening in the winter, fading in the summer.

Emilio clapped, and the attendant reappeared and escorted Kate to a chair where her hair was washed, wrapped, rinsed and wrapped again until she was judged ready to return to Emilio.

"Don't give me anything I have to set."

Kate wondered how a woman with wet hair and a spot on her

shirt had the courage to speak this way to an artist.

"What I am giving you," he emphasized the you, "is uptown butch. You won't need a thing but some styling gel and a blow dryer." He paused, looking down. "You do have a blow dryer?"

She nodded, silently promising that she would within the hour.

The attendant reappeared to offer both Emilio and Kate a glass of wine. Kate refused but Emilio took one, sipping slowly as he worked.

Another woman approached, pushing a table in front of her. "Will she want nails?"

She directed the question to Emilio, who shook his head. "Just work on the hands."

Emilio clipped and studied, clipped and studied until, abruptly, he rested his scissors on the counter in front of the chair and left.

The manicurist reappeared, lowering Kate's chair and positioning her so that one hand soaked in a bowl of milky white solution while the other rested passively beside it. The manicurist leaned over Kate's hand, humming softly to herself and looking like she was searching for fossils. Kate shifted uncomfortably.

After her hands were polished, trimmed and buffed, the attendant appeared to lead Kate to the cosmetician, a statuesque woman whose nametag read Sabrina. She placed Kate in a chair facing a mirror outlined in round, bright lights.

"You've got good skin, dear," she said, "and if you put a little blush here," she touched Kate's cheekbones, "you'll just heighten these and enhance your natural color."

Kate nodded as if she understood what she was being told.

She looked at the image in the mirror. Her hair was short on the sides and in the back, with slight bangs on the forehead, and a shade darker than when she walked in, almost auburn, with highlights that hadn't been there before. Her eyes looked larger, deeper.

"Just a little foundation," the cosmetologist said, as if she were thinking aloud. "And don't forget the lipstick." She said this as if she was warning Kate to remember some vital inoculation.

Emilio swept by.

"Get those lashes. She's got great lashes."

Obediently the cosmetician applied mascara until Kate stopped her. "I don't want to look like Tammy Faye Bakker."

At the end, she was led back to Emilio, who applied sweet-smelling substances, gels, and hot air to her hair, brushing and blowing. The attendant stood off to one side, waiting for an invisible signal, then she moved forward to untie the plastic smock.

"You're going to knock her dead," Emilio said softly in her ear. Kate smiled back at his image in the mirror. For an instant she let herself pretend there really was a her. It was a lovely thought.

She had one more stop to make. She drove to the bus depot and found the luggage lockers. She slid her wallet out of her pocket and pulled out the driver's license to lock inside. It was better to be caught with no identification than with the wrong identification.

CHAPTER NINETEEN

Back at the motel, Kate was too wired to stay in her room so she walked to the beach and dialed Gruber on her cell phone. After two rings she was greeted with a series of metallic beeps that made her hold the phone away from her head and stare at it. Then she remembered it meant he wasn't around, and she should punch in her own number to leave a message.

She tucked the phone back in her jacket and sat in the sand, watching the sun drop lower over the bay. Evening clouds were gathering over the Gulf and moving inland. She stood up and took a long, slow stretch, then tossed her head back, breathing deeply. This moment was full of possibilities—she had a new persona, new clothes. The money was going fast, but she still had enough to take off. Kate Porter could vanish, leaving her free to fabricate a new name with a history to match, just as she'd done during her years on the run. Even if she had to steal a dead child's name off a tombstone, she wouldn't have to hide at day labor jobs waiting to be arrested. She could get a passport, move to Guatemala, Belize, live on a beach, drink in mysterious bars, maybe even have love affairs with dark-eyed women.

The cell phone's insistent buzz brought her back. She filled Gruber in on her plan. He didn't like it.

"In the first place, some of those guys might know who you are. You get made and we're dead in the water."

Kate had to agree.

"In the second place, what are you going to do, buy yourself a truckload of guns?"

"So what if I do? Bud may hear about some woman down here

buying guns, get interested and come around to have a look. We just might nail him."

"That's really stupid, Kate." Gruber's voice was impatient. "Somebody'll just take a pop at you…" His voice trailed off. The unfinished part of the sentence was that he would lose his snitch.

"On the other hand, I might come up with somebody for your friend Charlie to pick up and squeeze. We could get some names." She paused to let that sink in. "You need some names."

"I've got—" Gruber started.

"You've got shit," Kate interrupted. "What you've got is some half-baked tax protester with three wives, who won't come off his property and a mama's boy who likes to dress up in uniforms. Bud's too smart to mess with people like that."

The phone was silent for a moment. Gruber sighed heavily. "What are you planning to buy from Mr. Thompson?"

"I thought I'd ask for a couple of cases of M-16s, then see if he'd be able to lay hands on some M-60s and some grenade launchers. That's just for openers—to check his merchandise and see how he does business."

Gruber cleared his throat the way he did when he disagreed but didn't want to fight. "You're talking a lot of money there. M-16s are going to run you a thou each. Hell, I don't even know what an M-60 goes for."

"I do." Kate said. The M-60 was the army's machine gun. When she went inside, they were going for around four thousand five-hundred each. These days they'd probably cost six thousand. Grenade launchers plus grenades should go for thirteen thousand dollars or so. However it added up, it should be enough of a sale to interest a wholesaler.

"They're going to want references," Gruber said.

"Can you help me there?"

"What name you using?"

"Nadine. Nadine Parker."

Gruber promised to make some calls but couldn't assure her of anything. Gruber never assured anyone of anything. They agreed to meet later at the park behind the library. There was some bird he wanted to look for that was supposed to be around there.

He was waiting by his jeep when she pulled into the parking lot. He'd been roaming the park looking for a grey silky flycatcher that he'd heard had blown up from Mexico. Another birdwatcher had told him it had been seen in town around dawn and dusk.

He did a double take when she got out of the car.

"You look different."

"Just playing the part." She knew different meant good.

Inside the park, Gruber walked slightly ahead, scanning for his bird.

"Any idea what we'll give them?" Kate was shading her eyes with her right hand, scanning the trees. A smallish bird with a tiny crest hopped back and forth in a live oak in front of her. The tomcat she'd seen earlier watched from the protection of a storm drain, but he withdrew into the shadows when he heard them talking.

"I phoned Topeka. There's a name you can use, J.T. Herrington."

"Who's he?"

Gruber sighed. "Mr. Herrington is a mortgage banker who likes to gamble. He got into laundering money for another guy, Sonny Vitale, in Kansas City."

"How'd you guys get him?"

"It seems Mr. Herrington liked to go to the Cayman Islands on business, and, of course, he needed his secretary along to take important letters. What happened was his wife found out the secretary was twenty-two years old and a runner up for Miss Overland Park. She had a little talk with the IRS." Gruber shook his head in sympathy. "Herrington folded ten minutes into the interrogation. He gave up everyone he'd ever done business with, including Mr. Vitale."

"Amateurs," Kate said, smiling up at him.

"They'll want a number." Gruber reached into the pocket of his jacket and extracted a scrap of paper with a phone number penciled in.

Kate frowned. "Won't people know he's rolled over?"

"Nobody knows yet. Topeka says he won't be used for at least another month. For now, he's officially at the Betty Ford Center working on his co-dependency."

They agreed to meet at Sam's. Gruber would arrive about nine and wait in the bar. Kate would follow around ten. The daylight was fading, and he was anxious to make one last search for the flycatcher.

"One more thing," he said. "You wear that transmitter."

Kate started to protest but he raised a hand to silence her.

"You wear it or I'm pulling the plug."

"You mean stick it up my ass, that's what you mean."

"If somebody decides to do something funny, I want a way to locate you. I'm not here to help you kill yourself. You wear that damn thing. I mean it."

Gruber rarely swore. Kate figured it was an artifact of his Baptist upbringing.

The tiny bird she'd been watching came to rest on a limb about twelve feet behind Gruber. It posed, as if it was waiting to be photographed, then it caught sight of the cat and took flight.

"I think I just saw your bird. Try that live oak over there," Kate pointed.

"Shit," Gruber said, grabbing for his binoculars and turning toward the tree. "You be careful!" he called over his shoulder, but his mind was on the bird.

Sam's tried very hard to look like an overgrown fishing shack perched on the edge of the channel between Padre Island and the mainland. The building was outlined in blue lights and surrounded by a parking lot the size of an airfield. Kate chose a parking space at the far edge so she'd be able to get out fast if she needed to. She made her way past rows of pickups, vans, SUVs and the occasional Cadillac. Clusters of people were hanging around the front entrance, smoking and talking, but none of them had the watchful eyes of bodyguards. Kate stood around as if she was waiting for someone to join her. No cars had followed her in and no one seemed to take any notice of her.

Inside, Sam's was just another cowboy joint full of smoke, noise and big hats. Kate glanced in at the bar, searching for Gruber. It took a minute to spot him, standing about mid-bar in a sea of western shirts and cowboy hats. She wanted to give herself some time to get the feel of the place, so she stopped in front of the cigarette machine and bought a package of Marlboros. By the time she glanced up, Gruber had turned so she could catch his eye, but neither of them gave a sign of recognition. Instead, she wound her way through line dancers in jeans and four-hundred dollar boots until she found a waitress.

"Can you point me at Frankie?" she shouted over the din. The woman nodded toward the end of the bar.

Kate edged herself between drinkers crowding the bar and waited until a bald-headed bartender asked what she was drinking. She shouted out her order, then motioned him close enough to see a pierce hole in his left ear.

"I'm looking for Joe Ray Thompson."

Frankie's eyes narrowed. She slid a folded fifty-dollar bill toward him before he had time to say he didn't know anyone by that name. Their fingertips touched as he took the money. When he glanced at the denomination, his eyes flashed.

"He's in the back dining room, third table on the left."

Two men sat at the table. One was large, with a Buddha-like belly and a thick, impassive face. The second was thin and graceful, with black hair slicked back from his forehead. He was dressed in a white western suit, and when he turned Kate saw he wore a pair of round sunglasses that gave him the look of a romantic hero from a silent movie.

She edged up to the table and cleared her throat. She kept her voice a few notes higher than normal.

"Excuse me," she said, "I'm looking for Mr. Joe Ray Thompson."

Two large men seated at an adjacent table stood up. One made a move toward whatever he kept under the armhole of his jacket.

The thin man motioned for them to sit down, but neither man acknowledged her greeting. The fat man sat back a little and folded his hands over his belly. They were little hands, with carefully manicured nails. The thin man smiled expectantly, as if she were going to say more.

"I was told I could find him here to do some business." Kate sounded apologetic for disturbing their important conversation.

"What kind of business was you wanting him for?" the thin man

111

asked. He spoke with the soft, insinuating voice of a small-town under-taker.

"I—I heard he could help me buy some equipment I need."

He pushed back from the table and stood up.

"My name's Jimmy Tyler." He waited a moment. "And you're?"

"Nadine Parker," Kate said hastily, like a good girl who'd forgot-ten her manners in the presence of such a charming man.

He pulled out a chair for her and Kate slid in. The place opposite her must recently have been occupied. A half-filled bottle of Canada Dry sparkling water and an empty glass sat beside a red plastic stir-stick embedded in a slice of lemon. A cloth napkin perched off to one side, waiting to be claimed.

Jimmy Tyler took direction of the conversation.

"I don't recall seeing you before, Miz Nadine."

"I'm from Kansas City." Kate kept her voice light and her smile in place.

"You're here at a very pleasant time of year."

Kate smiled harder. Jimmy sounded like the Chamber of Commerce.

Tyler and Thompson worked like a team, the one engaging her while the other sat quietly sizing her up. The fat man's eyes were nearly closed, and he gave no sign of listening, but Kate was sure he could have repeated every word. Jimmy leaned closer to her.

"Maybe you could tell us what kind of equipment you're looking for." He winked as if they shared an unspoken joke.

"Well, I'd like a few things for self-defense." She kept her voice soft.

"Very wise." Jimmy nodded. "What kind of things did you have in mind?" His tone skirted the edges of amusement.

Kate took a deep breath and began as if she were reciting a mem-orized list. "I'd like an M-60, at least two cases of M-16s and a grenade launcher with a dozen cases of ammunition."

Jimmy's eyebrows raised over the edge of his sunglasses, and he glanced at Joe Ray, who responded with a blink and an almost imper-ceptible nod.

"Exactly what was it you was looking to defend?" Jimmy asked.

Kate started to answer when the fat man spoke in her direction. "I'm Joe Ray Thompson." The voice rumbled from deep in his chest.

"Forgive me, Miz Nadine." Jimmy was touching her shoulder with his own. "But you sound a lot like someone from the Bureau of Alcohol, Tobacco and Firearms looking to set up a sting."

Kate's smile got wider. "I'd be real stupid to do that, because your smart lawyer'd hit me with entrapment in a heartbeat, and we'd get thrown right out of court."

Jimmy leaned back and gave her a paternal smile, as if she were a charming child reciting a poem.

"She's very good," he said to Joe Ray. Then he turned back to Kate. "Now why is it someone would send a pretty little thing like you down here to do a deal?"

Kate leaned closer and broadened her smile. "Because I been in the metal trade since I got out of diapers. My people figure anybody's going to deal bad shit will try right away with me. I spot junk and the deal's off. It's good business."

Jimmy raised his glass in a small toast.

"References?" Joe Ray rumbled. She could have been applying for a second mortgage.

Kate gave them J.T. Herrington's name and number.

"We'll get back to you," Jimmy said. The shades hid his eyes, but the mouth wasn't smiling, and the voice wasn't quite as playful.

There was a stir and Jimmy turned. A redheaded woman was making her way through the room. She wore a black dress that was suspended from her shoulders by two tiny straps, and she had the buffed and polished look of someone who spent a lot of time in gyms and beauty parlors. Although she kept her eyes on Jimmy Tyler, her smile said she knew most of the men in the room were watching her.

Jimmy rose in greeting, and the woman gave him a practiced look that told him he was the most important man in the world. He pulled out the chair opposite Kate to seat her.

Kate felt her chest tighten and a warmth in her throat. Any moment her hands would begin to shake, so she took the precaution of resting them in her lap, palm covering fist.

Jimmy turned to her. "Nadine Parker, I'd like you to meet my

113

fiancée, Sally Rushing."

The name was different, the teeth had been capped, and the face had lost some of its roundness, but that only gave it more depth and greater beauty than she remembered.

She was looking at Melissa McEvoy.

CHAPTER TWENTY

Trying to look relaxed and happy at a table with two men who could order her death as easily as they could order another drink was hard enough. To do it seated opposite Lissa McEvoy, or Sally Rushing, or whatever it was she called herself, was even worse. Kate told herself to keep the smile in place and not let the nervous energy flooding down the back of her neck make her legs shake. Breathe slowly, she told herself, move slowly. If Lissa says anything, stand up and make a commotion loud enough for Gruber to hear. He'll come in and maybe we can make a run for it. Before they blow your head off, a little voice inside her added.

Lissa sipped her sparkling water, stopping to admire it as if it were an exceptionally good year. Jimmy talked on—Kate couldn't have said about what—his eyes sliding easily between the two women. Joe Ray sat in silence. Glancing in his direction, Kate found herself grateful for him. He neither gave nor asked for anything.

When she began to think her legs might shake off her body, she decided it was time to excuse herself. With luck she could weave her way toward the ladies' room, then duck to the bar, grab Gruber and make it out a side door.

But when she stood up, Lissa rose to join her. "I'll just show you where it is, hon." And she gave a tiny wave to Joe Ray and Jimmy.

They made their way between crowded tables toward a door marked Cowgirls. Kate stopped before entering, considering whether she should just make a run for the kitchen. There had to be a back door. It would take Gruber a while to notice she was gone, but she could call him later to tell him what happened. Before she could bolt,

Lissa turned in her direction and motioned for her to follow. As if she were being pulled on a cord, Kate followed.

Lissa opened the door and strode straight toward a huge mirror overlooking the sinks. She placed her handbag on one and leaned in toward the mirror to examine her face. "So what is it that brings you to Corpus, Nadine?" Her voice had the artificial sweetness of someone making fun of a Southern accent.

Kate checked beneath the doors of the toilet stalls and found a pair of feet under the last one. The sound of a dripping faucet echoed off the tile walls. The woman in the stall zipped something, then rearranged something else.

"Just business." Kate rested one shoulder against the wall while Lissa examined her image, searching it for hairline cracks. Kate was close enough to pick up her scent. It was fresh and clean—bitter lemon.

Lissa pulled a lipstick from her bag and applied it; then she made a grimace with her mouth to check her teeth. Kate remembered a crooked eyetooth, but it had been straightened or capped. She looked for the other imperfections—the little scar beside the right eye was still there. She'd gotten that from the border patrol officer at Brownsville when she and whatever-his-name-was got busted for transporting weed. There was also a new mark—a fading bruise of a bite peeking over the top of the dress on Lissa's right breast. Kate couldn't take her eyes off the spot. It drew her, while at the same time the thought of Jimmy putting it there made her sick.

Behind them the toilet flushed. A faded woman with artificially blackened hair stopped at a sink, washed one hand, paused again to touch her hair, then left.

Lissa glanced toward the door. "When'd you get out?"

"Last week." Kate spoke slowly to keep the tension out of her voice.

"Where'd Nadine Parker come from?" Lissa's voice had lost the sweet edge, but her accent still wasn't the one Kate remembered. It was more like educated Texas, less like Kansas flatland.

"Same place as Sally Rushing."

"And now its payback time, right?"

"I don't want trouble." Kate spoke slowly and raised both hands in a gesture of surrender.

"You won't get any from me," Lissa turned to face her, "if I don't get any from you." But her lips were pinched in anger. She turned her attention to her handbag, laying out its contents on the edge of the sink.

"Here." Kate extended the unopened cigarette package from her pocket. Lissa looked at her distrustfully, as if the cigarettes might explode, but she took it anyway. Kate found the matches that had come with it and lit one for her. Lissa leaned forward for a light, then stopped herself abruptly, crumpling the cigarette and throwing it into the wastebasket.

"And you'd never want to make trouble for me." Lissa made it sound like an accusation.

"I didn't shit on you." Kate felt a surge of anger from her chest. "You were the one who walked off."

"You self-righteous shitheel. You left me hanging. We were supposed to be tight." Lissa focused on her handbag.

"That's right. We were so tight you had to go fuck Muriel Martinez." Kate leaned forward, thrusting her face at Lissa's.

Muriel Martinez had been flirting with Lissa for weeks. Kate didn't like it, but Lissa thought it was cute. On that last day, they'd come in from the dining hall arguing about whether to play cards or watch television. It wasn't a big deal, at least not to Kate, but Lissa had stormed off, and a few minutes later she crossed the dayroom and parked herself beside Muriel Martinez. Muriel draped an arm around Lissa's shoulder in a gesture of victory. Someone turned down the volume on the television and everyone stopped talking. Stealing someone else's girlfriend was the signal for a fight. Kate felt everyone watching her, waiting for her next move.

She'd always promised herself she wouldn't get into one of these things—jailhouse butches fighting and scratching over some stupid femme. It went on all the time, and it wasn't going to happen to her.

Then Muriel and Lissa started to the leave the dayroom. Kate found herself following. Someone—she hated to think she'd been the one—shouted, "Cunt." Muriel threw the first punch, and Kate was bringing her right arm back to counter when a hack grabbed her from behind. Two other hacks appeared. One pushed Muriel against the wall, the other cornered Lissa. One guard struck Kate from behind, then used his club to beat her to the ground. Once she was down, he kicked her until she curled up in a ball.

That little fight got her six months in administrative segregation. The official report said she'd started the fight, so Muriel and Lissa got off. Instead of three meals a day, she got two, and she traded in her orange coveralls for a paper hospital gown with a slit up the back. By the time she got out, Lissa'd been released, and Muriel had taken up with some new fish from Ohio.

Kate shook her head. Lissa leaned on the sink, both hands clutching the edge. She looked down at the drain. "So, what are you doing here?"

"Making a buy."

Lissa shook her head, resigned. "Oh sure, you're just down here doing business. You get out and jump right into the family business. You're as dirty as the rest of them."

"What's my family got to do with this?

Lissa sighed with disgust. "You're not trying to tell me you're in this alone, are you?"

Kate tried to sound as tough as she could. "Damn right."

"Christ, you're dumber than I thought you were." Lissa closed her purse abruptly and made for the door.

When they returned to the table, Jimmy had ordered a round of drinks.

Lissa set hers on one side and caught the waitress's eye to ask for another spring water.

"She's on this health thing," Jimmy said to Kate. "Don't eat no sweets, no alcohol, no red meat."

Kate smiled. "She's watching her weight."

"Shit," Jimmy said, "she's in better shape than I am. She runs five miles every single day. She's up and out at dawn, rain or shine."

"And she never cheats?" Kate said.

Jimmy grinned expansively. "You can catch her every morning. Straight out the front door toward the Naval Air Station and back."

Lissa gave him a hyperfeminine smile. "Do you good to run with me."

"That'll be the day." Jimmy winked at Joe Ray.

118

CHAPTER TWENTY-ONE

Kate was at the edge of the parking lot before she thought of Gruber, but even when she did, she didn't stop. All she wanted to do was get away. Jimmy Tyler and Joe Ray Thompson seemed to buy her story, but if she was wrong they'd be sending someone to shut her down. If they thought she was undercover ATF, they'd probably just fold up their operation for awhile. Feds, even undercover feds, were dangerous targets. On the other hand, if they thought she was local, all bets were off.

As soon as she pulled out of the lot, a car picked her up. She slowed, then accelerated, to see if it would keep pace. She thought she was doing a good job staying calm until her cell phone sounded, and the noise scared her so badly that she almost went off the road. She slowed down enough to answer it. It was Gruber calling from right behind her.

"I'm going to pull around. You follow."

She slid her foot off the accelerator, and the headlights pulled alongside, then in front. She followed him down the freeway far enough for them to be sure no one was tailing them. Gruber signaled an exit and she followed him through silent residential streets to the parking lot of a convenience store where he motioned her into his car.

Gruber pulled back onto the streets. In the dim light of the instrument panel, she watched his frown deepen as she told him about the evening. He drove and listened without speaking, nodding from time to time. She could almost see him memorizing the details. Then she got to Lissa.

"We'll get you out of here tonight. Charlie can put you on a charter to Dallas."

"She's not going to turn me over, Ray. She's got too much to lose."

"Sure she will. It'll get her a new diamond necklace or a fancy dress by one of those Italian guys."

Kate shook her head. "She's Sally Rushing now. She won't want him knowing she was in Lexington. Besides, she thinks I'm doing a deal."

Gruber looked straight ahead, saying nothing. He was weighing the risks, she knew that much. The question was which ones? If his worry was her safety, then he'd have her on that plane. If he was worried about the operation, he might risk it.

At length he nodded. "Okay, but I want you packing. You got that Walther you bought today, right?"

"Get me something else," Kate said, "I'd rather have a .38 special." She'd stopped trusting automatics when a .45 jammed on her during a target shoot when she was in high school.

Gruber nodded. "I want you wired, too."

"Ray, I'm not walking around with this thing up my ass all the time."

"I don't care if you hang it off your ear. You wear it."

He dropped her back at her car, and she drove home on side streets, taking corners slowly, stopping at each intersection. If anyone had followed her, she wanted to know about it, but the streets were still.

The Gulf wind had brought low clouds, and they hung over the gas flares by the Nueces River, picking up a red glow as if they were burning. Even with the wind coming from offshore, the smell of the refineries was as strong as an open gas jet. There was another one of those ANDERSON NOW billboards at the North Beach Exit. The letters jumped out to grab you—VOTE FOR ANDERSON NOW—BEFORE IT'S TOO LATE! Goddamn politicians, Kate thought. She checked her rearview mirror one more time, but the streets were silent and empty.

Back at the motel, she closed the heavy door to her room with a relief she hadn't felt since she left Lexington. Being locked in for the night could feel pretty good.

She paced uneasily between the bed and the picture window, turning from time to time to look at the bedside phone, half expecting it to ring. It didn't and she stretched out on the bed to watch the ceiling. When she first came to Lexington, an older inmate taught her the way to do easy time: When you walk, slow down; drink plenty of water every day; keep your head down in the dining hall; and get used to looking at the ceiling at night.

What took shape on the ceiling tonight was an image of Lissa McEvoy as she'd looked on the day she arrived at Lexington with a busload of transferees. The older inmates called them fish. Lissa's long red hair and runner's body made her stand out. Then there was the way her eyes flashed. Other than that, she wasn't any different than the other fish. They all arrived scared. They might be timid or tough, but they were all bone scared. Lexington was the big time and they knew it.

It was probably Lissa's way of laughing that did it. Kate found herself paying more than the usual amount of attention when Lissa was around. Wherever Lissa was, people seemed to be laughing and joking around. At first Kate was glad to run into Lissa, then she began putting herself in the right place to come across her, even though not a word had passed between them.

She did manage a smile when Lissa crossed her path in the line for breakfast. Once she even sat across from her at a long table in the library, but she took so long thinking of the right thing to say that Lissa left before she said anything at all.

New Year's Eve came. Another calendar down. Women got weepy and homesick at Christmas, but New Year's was as close to a party night as they ever got. A lot of the guards called in sick, so there wasn't much more than a skeleton crew on the second shift, and Kate's wing hadn't been in trouble so they could count on the hacks skipping the evening count and leaving lights out until somewhere past midnight.

Shabeeka from the laundry invited her around to her crib for a drink, meaning fermented potato peels distilled to an electric jolt of alcohol which Kate mixed with orange juice but Shabeeka took straight, in throat-searing gulps.

Around ten o'clock, Brenda, a former welfare official who'd shot her boss when he caught her embezzling funds, joined them. A few minutes later Lissa came by, and Shabeeka called her over for a drink. Then, just before midnight, Brenda passed out on the floor, and Shabeeka wandered off to find someone she wanted to talk to.

Kate sat propped against the wall on the lower bunk. Lissa was on the other end, leaning forward, elbows on her knees, holding a Styrofoam cup with both hands.

When she began to speak, her voice was so soft that it was barely audible. "I know you don't like me." Lissa looked at the floor as if she might be reading a script at her feet. "But I just have to say this anyway. I really want to sleep with you."

Kate sat up to be sure she was hearing this right. Lissa kept talking as if she were alone in the room. "And I don't even know why I'm saying this to you except I'm so drunk and it's really...hard—"

Kate touched her arm but Lissa kept on talking.

"—being around you—"

Kate leaned forward and put two fingers on Lissa's lips to make her stop talking.

Lissa looked up, surprised, so Kate leaned forward to kiss her. Lissa's drink spilled to the floor, but neither of them noticed. The first kisses were small, exploratory, but then they got deeper and longer.

Brenda snored softly. They pulled off each other's clothes and slid under the covers. By the time someone came to tell them Shabeeka had passed out in the corridor, they were sharing a cigarette and giving each other the looks people exchange after good sex. Lissa was on her back, and Kate was lying propped on an elbow stroking her hair.

She touched Lissa's cheeks. "I'm sorry my hands are so rough," she said.

"They're good hands," Lissa said. Taking the one touching her cheek, she kissed Kate's fingers.

And then it was too much. Kate was back in Corpus, looking at a white ceiling and lying on an empty bed. She hauled herself up and threw off her new clothes, then showered and put on a T-shirt, her old jeans and jacket, moving automatically the way she had the day she fought Muriel Martinez. A voice—the one she usually listened to—spoke in urgent whispers, saying, "You don't want to do this. This is really crazy." And she listened, but went right on putting her change in her pocket and making sure she had her room key. With one last look at the rumpled bed, she left, closing the metal door quietly, so she wouldn't wake anyone.

In the car, she unfolded her map and traced a route from downtown to the Naval Air Station, then made her way through pre-dawn darkness until she found the causeway leading to the campus. The bay was on one side of the road and a marshy pond on the other. She made a U-turn to face toward town, then parked on the gravel shoulder.

The sky grew lighter, and, one by one, the gulls filtered in. They were Franklin's gulls in winter plumage, which made them look as if they'd nosed around in a pit of ashes and gotten soot on their foreheads and around their eyes. The wind off the Gulf was fresh and gusty, rumpling their feathers as they sat on posts and rocks.

A white-suited runner appeared in the distance, keeping an even pace. At closer range, Kate saw red hair pulled into a ponytail. She stood next to the car and leaned against the door so she could be seen.

Lissa's pace didn't slacken as she drew closer. Her eyes remained fixed on the road in front of her. Aside from the crunch as her feet hit the gravel, the only sounds were the wind and the gulls. She passed Kate as if she were no more than a road sign. Kate turned to watch until Lissa vanished around a bend in the road. Then she lowered herself back into the car.

CHAPTER TWENTY-TWO

Kate parked outside the motel and poked on the beach, kicking at piles of sand and stopping to sail a rock across the surface of the waves. Gulls started gathering in the hope that she'd feed them. Their expectant cries made her feel guilty, so she headed toward the newest hotel on the beach and found the restaurant. The hostess, with the rigid perfection of a Barbie doll, took one look at her and shunted her off to a rear table out of sight of the paying guests. After breakfast, she sat on the beach until the sun made her sleepy. On her way back to her room she stopped by the motel office to pick up a newspaper. As an afterthought, she filled a Styrofoam cup from the complimentary-coffee-for-our-guests-only pot next to the registration desk and returned to her room.

She flipped on the TV. There was one thing you could say for Lexington—there was never a lonely silence. Someone was always there—even if it was someone you hated. People spent the better part of the day watching TV and arguing about whether to watch *Jeopardy* or *Inside Edition*. She'd promised herself she'd never look at the damn TV again once she got out, but here she was, behind nine-inch concrete walls, watching television on a sunny morning and drinking a cup of coffee that was almost as bad as the steam coffee they made in the wash house.

She flipped through the cable channels until an image forced her to halt—ornate gold letters on a field of royal blue. It was the logo of the Gospel News Network. The letters faded away and an overly warm male voice welcomed her to *The Christian News Hour*, with Dwight Porter.

The camera focused on two men seated in what was meant to look like a living room. One was in his mid-thirties and was tall enough that he needed to stretch his legs out in front of him. He had the open face and wide grin of a country boy. His suit was tight at the shoulders and thighs, as if underneath it he was modestly hiding the body of an athlete.

Her brother, Dwight, sat facing him in a wheelchair. It was always a strange experience seeing him on television. Something about him—too professional, too mannered—made her want to stand up and shout for him to stop putting on a show and come on home. Watching now, the feeling was stronger than usual. As the camera moved in for a close-up, she could see his carefully tailored blue suit with elegant French cuffs held by large gold cufflinks. Although his legs were shrunken and useless, he wore a pair of equally elegant boots in what she assumed was an effort to look down home, but his manner and gestures all said he knew he was one important son of a bitch.

He introduced his guest as Glenn Anderson, the Republican senatorial candidate from Texas, and led him through a series of questions about his childhood, allowing him to recite what seemed to have become the standard American political upbringing—poor but hardworking parents who never accepted charity, who attended church and pushed their children to achieve. An outstanding record as a high school athlete and scholar, followed by a college scholarship, all laced with heavy doses of prayer and capitalism. This must be the clown whose campaign paid for all those billboards and signs she kept running across.

All the while, an eight-hundred number flashed across the bottom of the screen as a reminder to viewers to call and donate money to the Gospel News Network. From time to time Dwight stopped the interview, turned to the camera and appealed directly to the viewers.

"God gave us a job to do," he said, looking directly into the camera, "and we need your help. Please dig deep and send us that check."

The camera shifted to a close-up of Anderson. Someone had taught him to look straight into the lens when he spoke, so he appeared to be addressing each viewer individually.

"I want to stop big government, greedy taxation and the wave of crime that threatens us all. I want to restore American values. We need to make Texas and America safe for our families." He stopped for two beats. "And I want to do it now—before it's too late."

Kate almost laughed out loud. This sucker was nothing more than a pretty boy reciting lines like a bad actor. How the hell could anyone take him seriously? What did Dwight think he could do, invent another Ronald Reagan?

The phone beside her bed rang, startling her. Gruber wouldn't use anything but the cell phone. She answered cautiously.

"How you doing Nadine?" It was Jimmy Tyler. Kate fumbled to find paper and a pen on her bedside table.

"Just fine. How're you?"

"Listen here." It wasn't meant to make her stop—it was just his way of starting a sentence. "We checked with Kansas City, and they say your Mr. Herrington is good people. They say he's off in some hospital. You know about that?"

"Yeah, I heard he was sick."

"They was also saying he was a friend of Sonny Vitale's. You know Sonny?"

Kate took a chance. "He doesn't spend much time with people on my level."

It must have been the right answer, because Jimmy continued. "Ol' Joe Ray's out of town for a couple days, and we can't do no bidness till he gets back." Jimmy emphasized the *bidness*. Kate was certain that when the chips were down the country boy routine vanished. "I thought maybe you was getting bored. Maybe you'd like to join us at a little party tonight."

"What kind of party?" Kate kept her voice soft—intrigued but noncommittal.

"It's a fund-raiser for a candidate—Anderson. I got me a bunch of invites. There's gonna be some ol' boys there you ought to meet."

"Will the candidate be there?" Kate was careful to keep her voice modulated. No excitement, no anticipation, no questions about Sally Rushing.

"Hell, he oughta be. They're hoping to get a hundred-thousand for his political action committee tonight."

Kate pulled the phone away from her face so Jimmy wouldn't hear her taking a deep breath. If Gruber were here he'd tell her not to do it. She heard his voice anyway, arguing that it was just too risky going in there alone. She should decline and wait until he could back her up in case things went wrong.

She answered him in her mind—We're not getting anywhere. Bud's not taking the bait. If there's big bucks around, he might show up. She waited just a moment before she spoke. "Sure. I'd like that."

"Tell you what, then, why don't you meet us there—say about eight o'clock. I'll get your name on the guest list."

This meant another trip into Corpus, which netted her a pair of black satin pants cut like Wrangler 240s, a black silk shirt and a black velvet vest trimmed in gold beads and sequins.

The address Jimmy'd given her was on Padre Island and turned out to be in a tract of McMansions built in styles ranging from French provincial to Southwest adobe. The developer had carved canals, giving each house its own dock. Powerboats in various sizes were tethered to the docks like large, docile pets.

The house was stucco, meant to look like an adobe monastery. Two men in blue suits and white shirts—the kind with extra-wide shoulders to accommodate carefully tended muscles—guarded the entrance gate. They stopped her car and checked her name against a list on their clipboards before nodding her through. She drove up a blacktop drive where yet another blue-suited bodybuilder with a walkie-talkie awaited. As Kate approached, he spoke into it, then waved her to a parking space.

The front door swung open for her before she could ring the bell. There had to be a closed circuit camera monitoring the door, but she couldn't see it. It was too bad Gruber wasn't there. He'd love a setup like this.

She entered a foyer, which opened into a living room dominated by a huge fireplace. The guests seemed to have divided themselves according to gender, the women occupying the couches and chairs, the men standing in a group around the fireplace.

Beyond the living room, Kate could see a set of glass doors leading to a pool and terrace decorated with colored lights.

A woman in a red dress appeared in front of her. "Hi, I'm Debbie Owens. I'm so glad you could come." She managed to insert three extra syllables in "come."

Her skin was tanned just short of mahogany, and her short dark hair was cut in a wedge style that had been popular in the '70s. Her smile radiated the practiced luminosity of a cheerleader, but she managed to make herself sound as if she'd been waiting all night for Kate to arrive.

"Thanks," Kate said and started to introduce herself, but Debbie Owens cut her off, taking her arm and leading her to the living room.

"They called from Amarillo about an hour ago. They're grounded by fog." She shook her head in mock bewilderment and took it for granted that Kate knew who they were. "Can you believe it? Fog, in Amarillo!" She raised her voice to punctuate the last syllables of Amarillo. Kate guessed she was referring to the candidate.

"Into each life a little fog must fall," Kate said. It was a lame joke, but by the time she'd finished saying it Debbie Owens had been claimed by a group of women seated on a white leather couch facing the fireplace.

"So they'll be late?" a silver-haired woman asked.

"Joe Bailey says they're going to call up the National Weather Service and threaten to cut their budget." She gave them all a smile that revealed two rows of perfect white teeth, the kind made of porcelain bonded to the tiny stumps of their enamel predecessors.

Her hostess looked as if she were preparing to spin away so Kate asked quickly if Jimmy Tyler had arrived.

"Not yet," Debbie called over her shoulder. "You'll know when he does," and off she went before Kate could ask what she meant.

The men at the fireplace stood with drinks in hand. Some were dressed western style, with heavy silver belt buckles supporting their paunches. Others were lean and trim and wore suits that fit like they'd been tailor made. All were middle-aged or older.

The women seemed to be drinking mineral water or white wine. Their ages ranged from early twenties to indeterminate age-battlers, but all had the razor-thin bodies and sculpted hair of women who spent major portions of their time taking care of themselves. Kate made no move to join them. Their very presence made her feel as awkward as a calf at a lawn party.

Drifting toward the fireplace, she overhead three men talking about the value of the yen and the euro. In the Texas she remembered, they'd have been talking about oil and cattle, but the oil patch had dried up and beef prices were falling. These were men of the new century who managed futures and cash flow and handled cash transfers without asking inconvenient questions.

Kate wandered out to the terrace. The crowd was a little different—the men older and the women younger. The men favored western suits in light colors, with darker dress shirts underneath. There were fewer women, but they were curvier and they were drinking whiskey. One woman, tall and dark-haired, wearing a spandex dress that fit her like plastic wrap, gave her a very, very warm smile. Kate smiled back, but moved on quickly before she could get trapped.

A bar and buffet were set up outside a poolhouse on the opposite end of the terrace, and the smell of barbecue wafted from a set of grills behind it. She took a deep breath and felt her stomach touch her backbone, but she made no move to eat. Better to stay hungry and keep her edge. She found her way to the bar and ordered a glass of mineral water from a white-jacketed bartender.

At a table close to the food and drink a Hispanic man sat, large and grey-haired, flanked by two equally large younger men—probably his sons. Kate stood to one side, sheltered by a huge succulent plant and watched. People came and went one by one, speaking to the older man like supplicants. He nodded from time to time but said nothing.

Then there was a current of motion by the double doors, and the red-dressed hostess shrieked in what passed for a friendly greeting. Jimmy Tyler and Lissa McEvoy had arrived.

Jimmy wore a navy blue western suit with a white Resistol hat, the kind priced in the three figures, which, in keeping with his country-boy image, he hadn't removed. But, in a gesture of social deference, the sunglasses he'd worn at Sam's were dangling from his lapel pocket.

Lissa wore a white satin pantsuit and a tank top that showed off the perfect muscles of her abdomen. Her hair was loose and free and, Kate guessed, fragrant. Hair you could bury your face in.

Jimmy waved her over. "Glad you could make it." He smiled broadly and turned, waiting for Lissa to speak.

She smiled brilliantly, professionally. "We're so glad you could come tonight." She could have been greeting a customer at a restaurant.

Kate nodded awkwardly, trying to find words, but none came. It was as if her years in Lexington had robbed her of the ability to make social conversation.

Jimmy took her arm. "Come on over here. I want you to meet some of the local boys." Lissa fell away and Jimmy led her to three men standing at one end of the bar. They were smoking cigars and talking football.

"This is Harry Sawyer of Lone Star Trucking, Tom Whitney from Coastal Concrete and Bobby Morrison, who's a lawyer."

"And don't make no lawyer jokes," Sawyer said.

"This is Nadine Parker—a friend of Sonny Vitale's."

Sawyer raised his eyebrows toward his balding head. "How's old Sonny doing these days? Still playing golf?"

"I don't know much about his golf game," Kate said, smiling, "but he still drives a mean bargain."

"That's Sonny, all right."

She smiled and nodded and the conversation returned to Texas A&M's chances this year. These were the kind of men who were accustomed to talking past whatever women were present, so she could smile and nod until a break came, then slip away if she wanted. And she wanted.

When she was free, she made her way to the second floor and through a series of adjoining bedrooms until she found one with a balcony overlooking the terrace. She leaned on a railing, cupping her drink in both hands, watching the reflections of the colored lights in the water. She tried to imagine her father in this setting, but couldn't. Maybe he'd started with people like this, but by the time they robbed the bank at Hutchinson he was an outlaw. Next to these fat cats, he'd look like a wild-eyed terrorist. He might be around town, but not in a place like this.

The voices from below blended with music from the loudspeakers, so she didn't hear anything behind her until she caught the scent of bitter lemon. When she turned toward the doorway, Lissa stood in it, frowning.

"You hiding up here?"

"Looking for someplace quiet."

Lissa moved closer and rested one elbow on the railing. She looked Kate over, sizing her up and not liking what she saw. "You're one self-righteous shit, you know that?"

This wasn't the voice she used in speaking to Jimmy, and Kate was pretty sure she didn't swear in polite company. She sounded like the old Lissa.

"What's that supposed to mean?"

"It means, why didn't you ever write back? You could have written," she emphasized the *written*, "even if it was just to say you hated me." Her face reddened slightly and the little scar above her eye grew lighter. "I sat there in Kansas City for six months waiting to hear from you. But you never even bothered to write back."

Kate turned so that her back was against the railing. "I never got any letters."

"I wrote you every fucking week for six months." Lissa's voice sounded as if it might break with anger. "I even wrote Fat Alice to see if my mail was getting through." She looked at Kate now, her eyes glistening and her mouth tightening.

"I was in segregation," Kate said. "Remember?"

"I remember, all right, but they deliver mail in segregation. Don't try to tell me they don't."

Kate looked down and shook her head slowly. "Just after you left, Murphy took charge of segregation." Murphy had a thing about Kate—hated her the first time he saw her. Kate had given up trying to figure it out. All she knew was he was bad news. "The only mail I ever got was a notice that my subscription to *Town and Country* hadn't been paid for." Inmates liked to use other people's names to send for free trial subscriptions, and Kate half-hoped Lissa would laugh about it, but she made a sound of disbelief instead.

Kate turned until they both faced the same direction. They stood in silence, looking off into the distance. After a moment Lissa spoke again, her voice very soft. "Not a single letter?"

"Nothing."

Lissa nodded slowly. She moved slightly toward Kate, her mouth softening. Kate felt her own shoulders relaxing—the first hint she'd had that she was tense. "What'd you write to say?" she asked.

"That I was sorry I was such a shitheel." The light from the pool cast a shadow on her face, and she was close enough for Kate to catch the scent of her hair. A wave of longing swept through Kate, and she caught the edge of the balcony to steady herself. "Right after I got out I saw it, just a clear as anything. I couldn't stand leaving you. I know it was stupid, but I didn't know any other way to do it." Her voice dropped off.

Kate was about to ask, And now? but she stopped herself.

As if on cue, they moved closer, standing so their shoulders barely touched.

"It wouldn't have made much difference," Kate said, very softly. "You'd still have had to leave."

"And you'd still have had to go to segregation." Lissa said. She glanced over at Kate, almost smiling. "You ever get around to clocking Murphy?"

Kate nodded.

"When?"

"He came after me in the dining hall, and I dumped him on his butt. It cost me another six in seg, but it was worth every minute of it."

"You got him right in front of everybody?" Lissa was smiling broadly now, her head tossed slightly back.

Kate nodded. It had been a wonderful moment. Murphy appeared behind her, shouting and ordering her to her feet. Kate had pushed back from the table, stood and, as Murphy approached, turned and landed a punch to the midsection that sent him gasping to the floor. Two other hacks grabbed her, throwing her down and yanking her arms behind her back so sharply she felt like they might pull out of their sockets. They bound her hands so tightly she lost all feeling in her left fingers for two weeks. But everyone knew about it, even people who weren't there. The whole time she was in segregation, they smuggled small gifts in on her food tray—two fresh strawberries from the garden, a branch of honeysuckle, half a Snickers bar.

Lissa had moved closer and Kate had the feeling that any minute now one of them would reach toward the other, and the invisible barrier between them would crumble. She pulled back slightly. This was no place for barriers to fall.

Lissa seemed the have the same thought. She looked away. Kate took a sip of mineral water, and they stared into the darkness, breathing the same night air as gently as if they were kissing.

CHAPTER TWENTY-THREE

After awhile Jimmy appeared. "I been looking for you girls."

Lissa turned to give him her smile, as if he were just the thing she needed to complete her life. "We've been standing here studying the ladies of Corpus."

"And what did you find?" Jimmy had his half-serious voice—the one people use to talk to children and small dogs.

"That we need a trip to that Neiman Marcus Spa up in Dallas, don't we Nadine?"

Kate was suddenly aware of the contrast between her own black silk, which bordered on tacky, and Lissa's expensive sheen.

"Then we'll just have to send you up there, won't we. Y'all come on down now. Mr. Anderson's here."

Downstairs, people had gathered in the living room. The candidate stood at one end, and the large Hispanic man with his entourage had placed himself strategically on a couch in front. When Jimmy noticed Kate looking at them, he leaned in and whispered, "That's Manny Gutierrez and his boys. He controls everything that goes on in Cameron County."

Kate nodded. If she remembered her Texas geography correctly, Cameron County was about four hours southwest of Corpus, on the border with Mexico.

The candidate stood to one side while a shorter man with the harassed look of a campaign manager moved in front and called for attention.

"I'm Joe Bailey," he said, "for those of you who haven't already met me." He paused to wait for the knowing laughter. Everyone there had met Bailey.

"I just want to say this is a private party, just for those of us who care what's happening to America. Now you know we're going to hit you up for money tonight." Another wave of soft laughter. "But I want our candidate to tell you why we need your help. Ladies and gentlemen," Bailey turned with a flourish, "I give you the next senator from Texas, Glenn Anderson."

Anderson stepped forward to vigorous applause.

"I think you all know this country is in trouble. We here," he gestured to include everyone in the room, "are business people—doing the kind of work that made this state and this country great. And what we need is a climate where business can work. We've got to put an end to government interference and regulation so we can get on with the job of keeping America first." He stepped back, smiling proudly, taking in the applause and the whistles. It was a short speech—just a soundbite. Maybe his handlers didn't trust him to say more, but no one seemed to notice. Except for the elder Gutierrez, everyone in the crowd stood up. Gutierrez, Kate thought, wouldn't stand up for the Pope.

Bailey circulated, collecting checks here and there. Kate caught a glimpse of Jimmy's—it looked to be five figures. Anderson should clear a hundred thousand without any trouble tonight.

When the party began thinning out, Jimmy suggested they go. Their hostess appeared and embraced Lissa, sprinkling her with air kisses, then holding her at arm's length to admire her. "I don't know how you do it. You look wonderful." Lissa gave her the smile younger mistresses reserve for the wives of their lovers' friends. "And thank you again for coming."

Debbie Owens turned to Kate as if she actually knew her. "We so appreciate your support." Then she was off.

Jimmy announced that he and Lissa were going for a late supper. Did Kate want to join them? She started to say yes, but Lissa shook her head imperceptibly and touched Jimmy's arm.

"Why don't we just go home, and I'll build you a sandwich. I've got to be up early for my run."

Jimmy looked apologetically at Kate. "I can't get her to hang out late anymore."

Kate walked them through the door and stood watching. Jimmy opened Lissa's door with a flourish, then rounded the car to take his seat behind the wheel. Kate watched until the taillights sped into the dark.

A blue-suited muscle man appeared behind her. "Can I walk you to your car?" Kate looked up at the expressively impassive face. He thought she was drunk.

"I'm fine," she said, and turned away, feeling him watching her steps, waiting for her to trip.

She drove through darkened streets searching for a bar, someplace with ribs and a great jukebox where she could drink until she fell over on her sorry ass. She was chasing the ghost of something that had ended a long time ago. Gruber was right to try and get inside the organization. She was just pissing around, wasting time.

She pulled over to one side of the road and stopped to punch Gruber's number into her phone. When Gruber answered, his voice was thick with sleep and he sounded hungover. He didn't want her to come to his place. He directed her to a parking lot on Padre Island.

A cold wind had cleared the evening mist, letting the half moon shine down on the parking lot. Gruber's jeep waited off to one side. He flashed his parking lights in greeting.

Gruber smelled of cigarettes and stale beer. His eyes were puffy and he hadn't shaved. He nodded dully as she recited her evening, even nodding in mild approval as she recited the guests' names.

But when she finished he said, "You shouldn't have gone without checking with me first."

Kate looked down silently, hoping he'd take that for an apology. "What've you got?" she asked after a few seconds.

"A shitload of hot air about the New World Order." He sighed heavily. "But Willie did let one thing slip. They've got some airstrips around here."

Kate frowned. "If there're airstrips they must be moving something that isn't weapons. You'd need something the size of a commercial airport to land anything big enough to carry weapons."

136

"Airstrips mean drugs."

She shook her head, uncomprehending. Bud had always been against drugs. He banned whiskey within the force and even rationed beer. A man could get kicked out of the force for admitting to smoking marijuana. She couldn't see him dealing drugs.

Gruber shrugged. "I don't know what to tell you. I'm going to phone a buddy with Alcohol, Tobacco and Firearms down in Brownsville. They keep an eye on traffic patterns over the border, so I want to see if he's got anything on flights around here."

Kate nodded slowly, still sorting out what she'd heard. It was easy to believe Jimmy and Joe Ray could be involved in drugs. It made perfect sense. They could bring a shipment in from Mexico, use some of it to trade for stolen weapons, then combine the rest with a shipment of weapons out of state. Any way you turned, you made money. But not Bud.

"You think I should go on with Jimmy?" she asked.

Gruber looked surprised. "I don't know why not. Whatever you get's gonna be good stuff. Charlie can use it. Maybe he can put the squeeze on your girlfriend."

Kate shook her head emphatically. "She's out."

"Not as far as I'm concerned."

"She's out or I'm out."

Gruber raised his hands in a gesture of conciliation. "I don't want to get you all lit up. All I'm saying is keep going. We're getting good stuff from this."

Kate regarded him steadily. At first he met her gaze and smiled slightly to reassure her. Then he looked away.

CHAPTER TWENTY-FOUR

In the three days that followed, Kate walked from one end of the Corpus beachfront to the other while she tried to work it out in her head. There was no way Bud would be working with drug dealers, even if they were the biggest gun traders in the Coastal Bend. On the other hand, these men did have a connection to Dwight, if only through that nincompoop candidate. The whole thing reminded her of a jigsaw puzzle where somebody had come through and recut the pieces so that nothing could ever fit again.

She ordered meals and left them uneaten, walked out of two movies, and spent the best part of two long nights flipping from channel to channel on the television, but she couldn't come to a conclusion. And when she let her mind go slack, it would fill with the scent of Lissa's hair.

Except for the occasional call from Gruber, she spoke to no one.

On the third day, she felt hungry enough to give food another try. She drove past rows of fast food places until she came to a taqueria that looked down and out enough to suit her mood. The waitress told her the fajitas were the real kind, made out of beef skirt and marinated forty-eight hours before they were fried with onion and green pepper.

She settled into a booth that gave her a view of the door. A rotund man in a dark suit and bolo tie appeared at the entrance and scanned the room. When he saw that Kate was the only customer, he headed toward her with the genial smile of a Baptist deacon.

"Are you Miss Nadine?" he asked.

"Just Nadine." Kate motioned for him to take a seat and gave him a lazy smile, one that promised more if he'd just be a good boy. She tried to look relaxed, but her legs were already electric with tension and her chest was getting tight. She hadn't picked up anyone following her. It was her slipup, and there was no chance now of contacting Gruber. She'd just have to play this hand out alone.

The man remained standing. "Mr. Tyler and Mr. Thompson would like to talk some business with you."

He waited by the door while she cancelled her order and gave the waitress a five-dollar bill for her trouble. Then he led her to a black van parked outside. He opened the door for her. A second man lounged in the back seat. He wore a white T-shirt with the sleeves rolled up to his shoulders to show his muscles. His jeans were tattered but his boots were new, and someone had tattooed three tears below the corner of his left eye. She recognized the symbols. Each tear stood for a man he'd killed—or claimed to have killed.

The deacon took the driver's seat and started the engine. He tuned the radio to a Christian music station. They left Corpus on the bridge to Portland, then turned north on the highway toward Sinton.

The two men talked like she wasn't there, arguing about high school football teams. Kate looked straight ahead, watching the divider strips in the road move toward her. She might be on the way to meet Jimmy and Joe Ray. Or she could be meeting her father. Or these two men might be taking her on a one-way trip to a ditch on a deserted country road. There was just no way to tell. The main thing was to stay cool and hope they couldn't see her knuckles getting white.

The deacon stopped at an abandoned gas station and pulled up beside a windowless delivery van. The younger man jumped out.

"We'll change vehicles here, Miss Nadine," the deacon said.

Kate got out and followed him to the rear of the second van, where the younger man waited beside the open doors. His face broke into a wide smile, revealing a missing eyetooth.

"We're going to have to search you now," the deacon said.

The younger man positioned himself behind her and wrapped his arms around her chest, pulling her against his crotch. Then he began to rotate against her.

"Just business," the deacon said apologetically.

139

Kate pulled herself free. "Then you do the search."

He paused for a moment, then signaled for the younger man to step aside. He knelt in front of her and patted her legs gingerly, as if she might catch fire and burn him.

When he finished, he pulled himself up with a grunt. "You mind taking your boots off"

Kate rested on the bed of the van, pulling off first one boot and then the other, handing them over for inspection.

"Can I check the jacket?"

She shucked it off and passed it to the younger man, who removed the cell phone and tossed it to the deacon. He extracted a knife from a holster on his belt and made a tear in the lining to reach inside and feel around. When he finished, he handed the jacket to Kate, smirking like a bad boy.

The deacon moved in again, this time checking her breasts, then her back and, finally, patting her butt.

"We're going to have to blindfold you now."

Kate nodded and turned so the younger man could tie a bandanna tightly around her head.

"Hands back," he said.

"What for?"

"Back." He seized both her wrists and jerked them behind her. She felt a plastic tie encircle them.

"Not too tight," the deacon said.

One of the men—the hot hands felt like the younger one's—pushed her inside the truck. She lay on the floor, wondering whether it was worth struggling to sit upright. If they were going to shoot her and dump her somewhere, it wouldn't matter whether she sat up or not, but she knew one thing, she was going to aim one hell of a kick for that sucker's balls before he pulled the trigger on her.

The combination of engine and road noise kept her from hearing any more conversation. Judging by the absence of traffic, they were on a farm-to-market road. She lost feeling in her left hand, and both arms felt like fire ants were crawling slowly up to her shoulder. After some time—she estimated it was half an hour—the van slowed and turned onto what felt like a gravel road. More time passed, then the van slowed and came to a stop. Kate heard the deacon speaking into a radio. "It's us," he said.

There was a pause, then the crackle of static.

"You're clear. Come on in."

The voice sounded like Jimmy Tyler's.

The van picked up speed, then slowed again and came to a stop. She heard both passengers get out, and seconds later the rear doors opened. Hands pulled her up and out to solid ground. One of the men, probably the deacon, loosened her hands so she could pull the bandanna off her eyes.

They were at the edge of a concrete airstrip, probably a remnant of World War II. The lone building was a rusting tin shed, which was unremarkable except for the fact that all its windows were intact. Looking at the strip itself, Kate noticed that it was in surprisingly good repair, the cracks filled with tar, and the brush grass trimmed just high enough to hide night landing lights.

The building itself was too small to be a major arms depot, but it would make a perfect place to unload and transfer other cargo—say cocaine or heroin flown across the border. The landing strip was heavy enough for World War II fighters, but it could never handle the weight of a modern cargo plane. Whatever they were landing here couldn't be any bigger than a four or six-passenger plane.

The door to the building rolled up to reveal Jimmy Tyler with his arms folded across his chest and his sunglasses in place.

"Boys give you a good ride?" he asked.

"Good enough."

Tyler turned away, and she followed him through a corridor made from stacks of long wooden crates with serial numbers stenciled on the sides.

Jimmy led her to a glassed-in office where Joe Ray sat in front of a metal desk littered with papers and ashtrays. The fluorescent lights gave his skin a yellow, faintly jaundiced tone. Jimmy put his hands on a chair facing Joe Ray, and Kate sat down.

"Want something to drink?" Jimmy asked.

Kate shook her head.

"Boys didn't shake you up?" Joe Ray said.

"I like dealing with careful people. Good business."

Joe Ray nodded as if she had uttered the wisdom of the ages.

He cleared his throat carefully. "We talked to Kansas City. They say Mr. Herrington's got deep pockets. So we thought maybe you'd like to see some product." He gripped the arms of his chair and forced himself up. With Kate and Jimmy following, he moved slowly toward the door, pausing to read the stencils on several boxes. Jimmy swept up a crowbar from the floor outside the office.

"Let's see." Joe Ray paused and looked around. "You were interested in some M-16s and," he turned back to Kate, "what else was it?"

"Browning .60 caliber and a grenade launcher."

Joe Ray frowned thoughtfully. "The Browning might take some time. You interested in some H&K semis? We could fix you up with some nice M-94s. They still got factory grease on them."

"They're nice pieces, but a little beyond our price range." Kate said. "We're looking for volume."

"That's your M-16, then," Jimmy said. "It's a hell of a workhorse."

Jimmy led her down an aisle of wooden shipping crates to an open crate on the floor. It was full of packages wrapped in heavy brown paper that smelled of grease. He unwrapped one package, revealing the disassembled parts of an M-16A2. Kate knelt down and touched the barrel. It was covered with Cosmoline. Joe Ray reached into his jacket and offered her a pristine white cotton handkerchief. She wiped the barrel and held it out to examine it. All the parts would have to be wiped down with WD-40 to clean off the thick brown cosmoline before they could be assembled. From the look of it, the goods were straight from the factory.

"They all in this condition?"she asked

"Every item fully guaranteed—money back if you're not satisfied." Jimmy could have been selling mouthwash.

"How pieces do you have available?"

"How many do you need?"

Jimmy pulled out a weapon that had been cleaned and assembled. Kate checked the action and aimed out into the distance.

Jimmy led her back to the little office. "The M-16s are no problem. We got plenty of product on hand. The grenade launcher and the Brownings could take a few days. If you don't mind foreign equipment, I can get you a Russian RPG-7 grenade launcher. We can do a partial shipment and backorder the rest. How many pieces was you thinking of?"

"Depends on what you want for them." Kate gave him her helpless-little-girl-trying-to-do-business smile. "What's your price for the M-16s?"

Joe Ray settled himself into a chair. His eyes flickered. He had no interest in guns—only money.

"Fourteen per piece." Jimmy was omitting the last two zeros.

"Wholesale?" Kate was into the game now. "I can take five dozen off your hands for eight per piece. Then we can handle two of the Brownings and the one RPG, but I would expect a discount for foreign. Your standard M-203 should go for around thirteen. I'd go maybe ten for a Russian."

"We're offering you wholesale prices," Jimmy said.

"And I'm offering you cash money. I can pay you two-fifty for five dozen M-16s, two Brownings and a Russian RPG. That includes one hundred and fifty rounds of ammo per piece with ten crates of grenades. My own truck will meet yours and do the pickup. You won't even be out gas and oil."

"We couldn't go any lower than three twenty-five on those."

Jimmy glanced at Joe Ray.

Kate ignored him and spoke to Joe Ray. "You've got a lot of product to move. I think we can help each other out."

They bantered back and forth a few minutes more, Jimmy doing the talking, Kate addressing Joe Ray. He came down to three-ten. She went up to two-ninety.

The air in the shed was getting close, and Kate felt sweat running down her back. She was going to have to stall things out or they'd want to see some cash.

Finally Joe Ray said, "We stay with three-ten. That's as far as we go."

Kate leaned back and sighed. "I'll have to phone Kansas City on this and get back to you."

Joe Ray nodded.

Jimmy walked back to the van with her. "Got to check this one out with the bossman?"

Kate gave him what she hoped was a sweet smile. "I always check with the money before I make the final commitment. It's good business."

She looked around as they walked, but she couldn't see a sign of anyone else hanging back in the shadows. It wouldn't be like Bud to miss out on the sales. God knows, he loved dickering around, and she couldn't imagine him leaving that to someone else, even if he was hiding out.

She paused before climbing back into the van. "You got a nice setup. Must pump a lot of money."

Jimmy smiled, not agreeing or disagreeing.

"Tell you what. If we can work something out, you get ahold of whoever's in charge of all this and tell him we'd like to talk about some of your other products."

Jimmy just smiled again and told the boys to give her a good ride home.

This time the deacon didn't bother changing vans. They returned Kate to the taqueria and left her in the parking lot, massaging her wrists. Overhead, high thin clouds had moved in, masking the sunlight and casting a veil over the dry palm trees that lined the lot. The smell of frying meat, peppers and onions made her weak with hunger. She went inside and ordered the same plate of food from the same waitress. When her meal came, she fell on it as if she were starved.

CHAPTER TWENTY-FIVE

It was a slow day at the taqueria, so Kate stayed at her table, ordering coffee she didn't want. She sat slumped over her table, trying to sort out the nagging questions provoked by her trip to the airstrip. The biggest was this: Where the hell was her father? Neither she nor Gruber had come up with anything remotely connected to him, but she was sure he was here. She could practically smell him. But, Christ! What was he up to? If he wanted to take her out, he'd had a dozen chances. She'd done everything but paint a target on her back. She set her cup down hard enough to make the waitress to look up from her *People en Español* magazine. Kate shook her head when the waitress started to get up and bring a towel. She pulled a paper napkin out of the holder and mopped up the warm liquid. Then she folded it up and slid it under the edge of her saucer.

The other thing eating at her was the feeling that the situation she found herself in was somehow all her fault. It all went back to that day at the University of Kansas when her father came to take her away. If she'd had the courage to turn around and walk away when he called to her, the robbery of the Hutchinson State Bank might never have happened. At the very least, it might have gone differently, and Viola McKinnon might still be alive.

Then there was the APF. The feds got a lot of convictions out of the information she gave when she turned herself in. All she'd wanted to do was plead guilty and do her time. She never intended to pour out all the rest about the APF, but once you started there was no easy place to stop. They pounded her with questions until, without meaning to, she told them everything she knew. She named names, supplied addresses, gave them phone numbers and secret mail drops.

"That's it, girl," she told herself, staring at her coffee cup. "You and your mouth. First you say nothing and then you say too much."

If she told Gruber she'd had a meeting with Jimmy and Joe Ray, she'd be setting herself up to snitch again. The next thing she knew, Charlie and his friends would pick Lissa up for questioning. They might even find something to charge her with. At the very least, she'd have to start over somewhere else. At the worst, Jimmy and Joe Ray would decide Lissa was a liability and her body would wash up on some beach somewhere.

The cook came out of the kitchen with a beer in his hand and took a stool next to the waitress. Kate glanced at the clock. It was getting late. She paid her check and stood in the doorway, watching a smear of clouds pushing in from the north. The wind had been from the south most of the day, but now it was shifting. There was going to be a change in the weather.

She got in her car and turned the radio to a Spanish pop station—great beat even if she couldn't understand a word. The best thing she could do was pick up her stuff and clear out of town right now. She didn't owe Lissa anything. Shit, the woman had humiliated her when she walked away at Lexington. Gruber and Charlie had enough on Joe Ray and Jimmy to pull them in for questioning. They didn't need her for that.

"Piss on it," she said aloud. All she had to do was call Gruber and tell him she was out. She could pull over right there and make the call. But her hands stayed on the steering wheel and she kept on driving. She'd snitched once. Jimmy and Joe Ray would take a fall, but they were players. They had connections with the local police, or a sympathetic judge, maybe even a senator-elect. They'd pull all the strings and buy all the lawyers it took to get off easy. She flashed on the television screen back at her motel—Dwight interviewing that fellow Anderson. It was remote, but there was a possibility that Jimmy and Joe Ray were on a line that led to Dwight. The thought made her stop short. She hated Dwight's politics, his sanctimonious, oozing pronouncements, but he'd stood by her. She owed him.

She found a pay phone at a Texaco station across the highway and called Dwight's number at the Gospel News Network. It took her four underlings to get through to his administrative assistant, the venerable Mary Lou.

"Katie," Mary Lou said, "how are you?" Her voice fell somewhere between dismay and concern.

"Can I talk to Dwight?"

"I can't disturb him."

"Mary Lou, I'm not kidding. This is really urgent."

Mary Lou made sounds of helplessness. "He's off on a spiritual retreat in North Carolina. There aren't any phones, but he calls in once a day for messages. Can I give him your number?"

"Oh shit," Kate said.

"Are you in some kind of trouble?" Mary Lou's voice got a little harder.

"Not me, but maybe him. Listen, isn't there any way I can talk to him?"

"Hon," Mary Lou's voice softened again. "You could e-mail him. I know he checks his e-mail once a day."

Mary Lou wouldn't let her off the phone until she promised to call back after she talked to Dwight. "I just worry about you, hon."

Kate lied and said she'd call.

She wasn't sure where to start with e-mail, so she drove back to the store where Gruber bought their cell phones. The nerdy salesman was out for the day, but a soft-faced man directed her to Kinko's, down the way, where a dark-haired girl with the kind of eyes you could drown in led her to a computer, helped her open a Yahoo account and get a screen name.

Kate wrote Dwight:

Hey D, I'm down here with some people trying to corner Daddy and we've run into some problems. There are these two guys, Jimmy Tyler and Joe Ray Thompson, who are into some heavy stuff. They're going to take a fall, and it might come back to bite you because they're contributing to the Anderson campaign. You might want to do something to cover your butt.

That said, she should have signed off. But there was something so conversational about the medium that it loosened something inside her. *"D, I have to tell you, I am scared to death. I keep thinking Daddy's watching me, waiting to jump out at me. I came here to find him, but I'm scared he's going to find me first. So whatever happens, watch your back, D."*

She signed it *"K,"* then went back and inserted *"Love, K."*

CHAPTER TWENTY-SIX

Back at the Sandy Shores, she spent the night pacing in front of the window. She closed the mustard colored curtains, feeling like she was going into lockdown. Finally she fell asleep in front of the television, lulled by a black and white movie starring Robert Mitchum and Jane Greer. It was about betrayal.

At four A.M. she woke, as completely as if the alarm had rung. The television news was on, and one of those animated Barbie dolls who read the news and weather was posed beside a weather map tracing the southward movement of a cold front from the Panhandle.

"And it looks like we're in for a cold day in the Coastal Bend." She sounded as happy as if she were announcing the lottery winner's name.

Kate pulled her blue suitcase from under the bed and began stuffing her new clothes inside. She thought about leaving the Walther. Who the hell needed to get picked up on a weapons charge? But she decided to throw it in. You never know when you'll need it. She hesitated again when she came to the leather jacket. But she decided to leave it out to wear.

Downstairs, she opened the trunk of her car. She didn't care if someone was watching. Gruber would check in later and find her gone. She could almost hear him yelling in her ear.

"No way," she said, pulling the door closed.

"It's off," she told herself as she slid behind the wheel.

There were a couple of things to take care of before she left. She'd need to collect her identification, just in case she got stopped somewhere along the way. And there was Lissa. She drove to the causeway connecting Jimmy's house on Ocean Drive to the Naval Air Station. If Lissa was running this morning, this was where she'd be.

It was still dark when she arrived, but the car felt cramped so she got out and kicked at gravel until the sky began to lighten. The breeze off the bay was fresh and damp, carrying just enough fog to dim the lights of the Naval Air Station, which lay beyond.

She crossed the road to look into the tidewater pool on the other side. Sunrise turned the heavy clouds over the Gulf a brilliant red, and gulls began descending silently, first one, then in twos and threes.

A solitary coot glided past a frail-looking shorebird on tall, thin legs. It was a delicate bird, white and grey, with a fragile neck. Kate mentally paged through her field guide—it was an avocet. Just then it moved, breaking the surface of the water to seize its prey.

A runner appeared out of the gloom. She caught a glimpse of emerald and white. As the figure drew closer, she saw it was too heavy and slow to be Lissa. Minutes later a middle-aged man passed on the other side of the road, eyes down, face straining with exhaustion.

She shivered in the breeze and crossed the road to her car. Just as she opened the door a hand touched her shoulder lightly. She turned to find Lissa running in place. "Run with me," she said, and when Kate hesitated, "my car's up there." She pointed toward town.

Kate fell in behind, her calves stretching and her knees protesting as the roadside caliche crunched beneath her feet. The Women's Prison Camp shared a track with the men's prison, but she hadn't run for months. At first, she was able to keep pace with Lissa, but after a half mile or so, she slowed down. Lissa slacked off, trying to allow for her.

"How far?" Kate wheezed.

"Just a little way up here." Lissa nodded her head. She wasn't even winded.

Kate forced herself on until they reached a silver BMW. Lissa leaned against it to stretch her calves, then she stood upright to stretch her arms and shoulders. Kate threw herself against a fender, gasping for breath.

Lissa bent to stretch her back. "You need to get in shape."

"That's what everyone tells me." Kate waited until Lissa clicked a little black button on her key ring to unlock the door for her.

"That looks like something out of a James Bond movie," she said, lowering herself gratefully into the seat.

"You been inside too long, girlfriend," Lissa said.

They drove to a taqueria on South Padre Island Drive—a tired looking place with a neon sign that said OPEN. The parking lot was nearly empty, but a minute after they pulled in a grey Camaro parked at the far end of the lot. The driver was on his cell phone and looking at a map propped on the steering wheel. There was something vaguely familiar about the shape of his head. Kate started to open her door so she could have a better look, but Lissa stayed in her seat looking straight ahead as if something might appear on the hood of the car. "Was what you said the other night the truth?"

Kate answered carefully, as if she were calming a frightened animal. "Every word."

She waited a moment before proceeding with a question of her own. "Those letters you talked about. Is that what you really wrote?"

Lissa nodded.

"I'm sorry I didn't get to read them."

Lissa shrugged. "You were right, though." She put both hands on the steering wheel and gripped it tightly. "It wouldn't really have made any difference." Her voice grew harder. "You were still going to be in there for four more years." She looked at Kate for the first time. "For all I knew, they'd get you for something else, and it'd be longer than that. Anyway, I just figured you got someone else."

"I didn't."

"Don't try to tell me that." Lissa tossed her head impatiently. "I've been inside."

"Did you get anyone?" Kate asked.

"I had a couple of things with girls." Lissa shook her head as if to throw off the memory. "It was okay, but it was just too close, you know?"

Kate nodded, remembering her own short affairs—one with a new inmate from Milwaukee, and the other, more painful, with an older woman, a former member of the Weather Underground who'd turned

151

herself in after years in hiding.

"How many?" Lissa persisted.

"Just a couple." Kate shifted uncomfortably.

"For real?" Lissa's hands loosened on the steering wheel.

"Some new people came in. I had some friends, but no more lovers."

"I'll bet," Lissa said, but the atmosphere in the car softened and Lissa gave her a little smile, the one Kate remembered from their first night together at Lexington.

They went inside and picked a quiet booth. When the waiter appeared with menus, they ordered huge breakfasts, as if the food might prolong their good feelings.

"And bring up a whole pot of coffee," Lissa called after him.

Lissa sat with her back to the wall, legs stretched out on the seat beside her. Kate hunched forward on the table. This was the moment they'd talked about at Lexington—the time when they were outside, free to do anything they wanted. Kate reminded herself she should be saying goodbye, bailing out before the conversation got serious. But she couldn't make herself stop smiling. "What'd you do when you got to Kansas City?" she asked.

"I waited tables for awhile." Lissa smiled at the memory. "It was nothing but guys hitting on me so I thought I better make some money off it. I decided I wanted to go to school," she shot Kate a look, "just like you always told me. I got on with an outcall service and enrolled at the University of Missouri, Kansas City."

Kate worked to keep a frown from forming. The university was good. The outcall service was not but she nodded in approval anyway.

"I took courses days and worked three nights a week. It paid the bills. Then I met this older guy. He wanted to set me up, so I did it. I saw him two nights a week, he paid the rent and a little extra and I went to school. He liked it that I was in college."

"Was he—?" Kate stopped herself, unsure of how far to go.

"Oh, he was okay, just straight sex. Nothing weird. But he had a heart attack one night, you know, in the act." Her gesture conveyed an image of a large bird crumbling in mid-flight.

"*In flagrante delicto*," Kate said.

Lissa made a little grimace. "I called his son before I got the ambulance. I mean, he was already dead. I didn't want to upset his wife." She sighed. "The family was grateful. His son—he gave me a little cash and I decided to move on to Dallas. I met Jimmy and here I am."

"And its great," Kate said.

"I'm working on a B.A., saving money like crazy, and living like a queen." Lissa looked guarded.

"And Jimmy?" Kate knew this kind of question wasn't going to help.

"He treats me okay. Well, you saw. It's okay."

"Right, he just deals guns and God knows what else. I guess that's okay." It wasn't what she should say, but she couldn't stop herself.

Lissa pulled herself up, ready to fight, then unexpectedly burst out laughing. "Well, shit, Katie, I guess he's better than the fella that got me sent to Lexington. He wanted to sell me to a Border Patrol dickhead to get himself off."

Kate laughed too. They'd both heard of worse.

"Actually, I'm very proud of you," Kate said, reaching across the table to take Lissa's hand.

"Proud?" Lissa wrapped her fingers around Kate's wrist, touching the veins with her index finger.

"You're getting a degree. You straightened yourself out. You're doing okay. Yeah," Kate surprised herself by what she was saying, "I'm proud."

Lissa gave her a self-deprecating smile.

The waiter appeared with their food, forcing them to move coffee cups and creamers. They both pulled back and concentrated on their plates.

Lissa rolled eggs in a flour tortilla. "So how's Shabeeka and the laundry crew?"

Kate told her about Shabeeka's death.

Lissa put her tortilla down, slowly. "And that little woman?" She groped for the name.

"Tracy," Kate said. "Her too. Pneumonia."

"Christ." Lissa looked off into the distance and set her jaw like someone struggling with tears.

"There were some other things." Kate wanted to change the mood. "We got a new warden in and she wanted to make the place pay for itself, so she decided to get us into telemarketing. They brought in all these computers and one of the trustees broke into the social worker's computer because it was connected to the Internet. By the time they caught her, she'd figured out how to bust a code to a credit organization, TRW or something like that." Kate glanced to one side to see if anyone could overhear. Lissa was smiling now. "She put the cop who arrested her, the judge who sentenced her, and her third grade teacher into twenty-one thousand dollars of paper debt with their credit cards."

"I love it." Lissa laughed.

"Last I heard, she was working on a way to get into the Justice Department computers. She wants to change her sentence."

"Did she get anything for herself out of all this?"

"A free lifetime membership in the Columbia Record Club, six sets of bone china, and a prospectus from a nursing home corporation in Florida."

Kate lifted the pot to pour coffee and found it empty. Lissa gestured to the waiter to bring another.

People were coming and going around them. Grizzled men in western shirts and jeans slid into booths, silently ate their eggs, and stared sadly into their coffee cups, lifting them for a final gulp before heading out to their pickups. The waiter went back and forth to the kitchen, emerging in bursts of greasy steam. Kate and Lissa were an island in their midst.

"Did they keep you working in the laundry?" Lissa asked.

"Up to the last day I was there. But I got some business going. I talked the assistant director into ordering new mangles and steam presses and I started me a nice little dry-cleaning business."

"With the fish," Lissa said, meaning the new prisoners.

"With everybody." Kate told her about the trade she'd developed to cater to the universal prison craving for clean, ironed sheets and sharply creased overalls.

"I traded Johnson, the new chief hack, a year's worth of dry cleaning for tickets to the University of Kentucky basketball series.

Shabeeka helped me sell them to the delivery guy who brought bread. He brought us two ponies of beer for New Years Eve." Kate laughed at the memory. "We had one hell of a party that night. People were just shitfaced."

"And you went to bed with who?" Lissa said, remembering an earlier New Year's Eve.

Kate shook her head and held up her hands defensively. "I went to bed alone."

"So where's your probation officer?" Lissa's voice grew serious.

"I'm off paper," Kate said. Her sentence was finished. She had no parole time to serve.

"How'd you swing that?"

"Got transferred to Lansing." That was the Kansas State Prison for Women. "They took me off paper and cut me loose. I'm a free woman." Lissa looked impressed, but Kate noted a slight dilation in her pupils. Somewhere she'd detected a lie. Kate braced herself for more questions, but Lissa talked instead about the classes she'd taken—the books she'd read, the debates she'd led. Teachers she hated, teachers she loved. She talked about discovering Baroque music, Lawrence Durrell and Adrienne Rich.

And Kate told Lissa about the sunrises she'd seen at Lexington, the nights she'd tracked satellites across the winter sky during the dark of the moon, and all about the woman who raised baby starlings on pureed chicken.

The restaurant cleared and filled and cleared again. Finally Lissa glanced at her watch. "I've got a class."

On the way back to her car, Kate was trying to say goodbye. Something casual and light, like, Hey, babe, I'm sorry. I was just passing through here looking to find my old man and rat on him. I didn't mean to run into you so I'm leaving town before I have to rat out your boyfriend and his business partner. But the words weren't coming.

The grey Camaro was still in the parking lot, and they passed close enough for Kate to get a good look. The front fender had a rusting gash in it that no one had bothered to fix. The license plate had a bracket with a silly little roadrunner on it. And then there was the driver—he looked a whole lot like the tattooed jailbird who'd helped the deacon take her to Jimmy's airstrip. She glanced at Lissa uneasily.

"Jimmy ever have you followed?" She nodded toward the grey Camaro.

Lissa gave a disgusted frown. "He likes to think I need a bodyguard when he's not around." She left Kate and walked to the Camaro. She leaned over and spoke to the driver for a moment, then returned. "I told him I was heading back to the house for the rest of the day. He'll leave us alone now."

Lissa drove her back to her car. Kate started to open the door to leave, then stopped and cleared her throat. She started to speak, but Lissa interrupted her. "Jimmy's gone tonight. You want to get together?"

"I don't know," Kate said slowly. "I may be tied up."

"Business?" Lissa's voice was light, but her eyes looked hurt.

"I'm not sure." Kate looked away.

"I've got a place out at Port Aransas. You know where that is?"

Kate nodded dumbly and let Lissa give her directions to the house. The key was under a flat rock just to the right of the front steps.

"I'll be there after six-thirty, so come on out when you get through."

Swiftly, too quickly for Kate to have anticipated it, Lissa leaned across and kissed her gently. Kate kissed back, wanting to hold on longer. It was Lissa who pulled back. "See you tonight." Her voice had a little catch in it.

Kate couldn't speak at all. She hauled herself out of the car and stood in the late morning sun, watching Lissa's car drive toward the college. She waited a few minutes longer to see if the grey Camaro appeared, but it was nowhere in sight.

CHAPTER TWENTY-SEVEN

Back in her own car, Kate flipped through radio stations to see if something could take her mind off what a shit she was. Gruber and Charlie would pull Jimmy in, Lissa's life would be turned upside down, and Bud Porter would be as free as a bird. She hit the steering wheel with her fist. For all the good she'd done she could have stayed in Lexington and gotten herself shanked.

She glanced into the rearview mirror. A grey Camaro appeared two cars back, behind a Ford Escort. She drove for several blocks, letting it hang behind. When the Escort turned off, she slowed until it drew close enough for her to see the outline of a roadrunner on the license plate bracket. The bodyguard had decided to follow her. There wasn't a single reason why Jimmy Tyler should be looking after her, so something else had to be going on. She went on a few blocks, then shot a quick left onto South Padre Island Drive. The Camaro followed.

Up ahead she saw a billboard advertising the Corpus Christi Mercado. An arrow of dancing white lights pointed toward an enormous converted warehouse. Kate cut in front of a Taurus that was signaling an exit. Through the rearview mirror, she saw the Camaro trying to follow, but the Taurus cut it off. She headed away from the Mercado until the Camaro was out of sight, then she made a U-turn and returned to the Mercado's packed lot. Just as she was cruising down a parking aisle, a beaten-up old pickup pulled out and she seized the space. If there was enough of a crowd inside, she could make it out a back door and leave the Camaro waiting in the parking lot.

The inside of the warehouse was a traditional Mexican market. Space was divided into tiny stalls selling everything from fresh produce to funeral caskets. Merchandise overflowed into the narrow aisles, and people milled around, sorting through piles of fabric, bargaining for jewelry and leather jackets, while Tex-Mex music boomed in the background.

A crowd was always a good place to hide. All she needed to do was browse, keep her head down until she could find a side door, and be out of there.

She was making like she was looking through used cassettes and compact discs when a cluster of teenagers came toward her. The leader was a large boy who used his size like a bulldozer clearing a path for the two boys and one girl who trailed behind. It was the girl who caught Kate's eye. She had dark hair, short and parted on one side so it dropped over her forehead. She had shoplifter eyes—the kind that saw everything. Kate watched her move to one side of the large boy so that he blocked her from the vendor's view, then slip four cassettes into her jacket. She looked up in time to catch Kate's eye. Kate smiled slightly and nodded in recognition but the girl slid off down another aisle.

Moments later the group passed her from the other direction. This time the girl met her gaze and looked her over carefully. For a minute it felt like she was being cruised, but the girl looked too straight for that.

A buzzing sound caught Kate's attention and she followed it to a tattoo booth. In full view of passersby, a woman was seated in a chair, leaning forward to rest her arms and chest on a table. She wore a surgical drape that exposed her left shoulder. A thin, grey-haired man bent over the shoulder, drawing the image of a rose in her skin. A man, probably her boyfriend, stood off to one side holding her jacket. He looked as if he might be sick any minute.

The air was close and the sight of beads of blood on the woman's arm made Kate a bit queasy too. She leaned on a pile of bath towels and watched the needle making a dark line. Streams of sweat formed in the small of her back. She pulled off her jacket and folded it under her elbows.

A man passed by wearing a black satin bomber jacket with the words Red's Taxi Service stitched on the back. It gave her an idea.

"Hey, Red," she called out.

"Yo."

She took a step in his direction. "You working?"

Red nodded.

"You want to drive me to Victoria?" It was a small town and not far away, but it would get her out of town, and she might be able to hitch a ride to Houston. From there, she could figure out where to go next.

"Right now?"

"Right now."

"Honey, I'll drive you to hell long as the meter's running."

Kate turned to grab her jacket but it was gone. She looked around, confused. She was sure she'd put it on the pile of towels. There hadn't been any movement around her. It couldn't have fallen. Then she remembered the pack of kids. She hadn't been what the girl was cruising—it was the jacket.

The man from a booth selling Guatemalan jackets and dresses crossed the aisle to her. "They took your jacket. I saw them." He smiled apologetically.

"Gotta watch 'em every minute," Red said.

"They come across the border, steal everything they can, then get caught and sent back." The man shook his head sadly. "I can give you a good price on a new one." He pointed toward the rows of patch-work bomber jackets hanging in two tiers at his stall.

Kate shook her head. It was warm enough to do without a jacket. She turned to Red. "Let's do it."

He shrugged and followed.

Suddenly there was a noise from the front of the building, and people streamed to the front door. Kate found herself caught in a surge of people moving forward. She turned to look for Red. "Give me a minute," she called over her shoulder.

As she reached the door, a man shouted, "Someone's down!" and a woman screamed.

Making her way to a door, she got a view of the parking lot. People crouched in the shelter of cars or lay flattened on the pavement, trying to make themselves invisible. Kate pushed her way past a man blocking the entrance and squeezed through the crowded doorway out into the parking lot. Someone behind her was shouting, "There's a shooter out there."

A space had cleared in the middle of the parking lot, between the lanes of cars. Kate saw a slim body on its back in a spreading pool of blood. She recognized the shape and the hair, but mostly she found herself looking at the black jacket with silver buckles. The girl must have ditched her own jacket and put Kate's on.

A man came out from behind a car and knelt at the girl's side. He lifted her hand searching for a pulse. From behind her, Kate heard someone shouting, "Don't move her."

The man raised his head slowly, and Kate felt as if he were looking directly at her. His face was thin, leathered, with the worried eyes of a man who'd seen too much pain. He shook his head. It was already too late.

Kate crossed an aisle of parked cars to come closer. The bullet had entered through the girl's forehead. Her lips were slightly parted and the eyes that saw everything were open, with a look of surprise. She seemed much younger than she had inside the Mercado. Kate knelt down and lifted the girl's hand. It lay in her own, warm and supple, but undeniably dead.

Kate stood and scanned the periphery of the parking lot. People were moving cautiously now. She heard sirens in the distance, but no vehicles were racing away. A sniper had picked out the jacket, taken aim at the head and faded away. It would have been an easy shot.

A police car arrived and Kate allowed herself to be pushed aside. She saw Red standing at the Mercado entrance on tiptoe, searching for her, so she made her way to him to say she wouldn't be going to Victoria.

Back at her own car, she stood looking into the distance where the shooter must have taken aim. If it was Jimmy's man, then her cover had been busted. Gruber had told her that Herrington was getting ready to turn evidence, but that information wouldn't be public yet. But there might have been a leak from inside. If Jimmy got the news about Herrington, he'd off her in a heartbeat. In his line of work it was called risk management.

But maybe the shooter had been her father's man. She shook her head at the thought. In the first place, he wouldn't have someone else do a job on his own daughter, and in the second place, he'd have known he had the wrong person in the crosshairs.

Kate jammed her fists in her pockets. If it hadn't been for her, that girl would be alive. She was goddamned if she was going to cause any more deaths. If Jimmy had ordered her hit, then Lissa was in danger and had to be gotten to a safe place. Her life as Sally Rushing would be over, but she'd be alive to make a fresh start. She could stop off and pick up her identification, then get out to Padre Island. There was a ferry to Rockport that would leave her on the road to Houston. Lissa would pitch a fit, but, Kate told herself, better a fit than a funeral. This time she was going to do the right thing.

CHAPTER TWENTY-EIGHT

All she got when she dialed Lissa's cell phone was a tinny little voice telling her the subscriber was not available, so she tried Gruber. No answer. At the next stoplight, she dialed information and got the sheriff's offices. When she asked for a deputy named Charles, the woman on the other end told her Deputy Watson was unavailable and asked if she wanted his voicemail.

Heavy clouds had moved in from the north, and the wind was shifting to the west, becoming decidedly cooler. Things were starting to feel unstable. She made a turn at the next corner and headed out toward Padre Island.

Lissa's house was on a street of beach houses that ended at an immense sand dune. All the lawns but hers were immaculate. Several had powerboats on trailers parked under carports. Lissa's place was a faded blue bungalow with a front yard turned into a beach garden of native rope grass and prickly pear cactus. It suited the sandy soil, but looking up the street at the carefully tended lawns, Kate could only imagine that the neighbors disapproved of more than the grass, if they knew.

She pulled into the driveway and scanned the street for the small shift of curtains, the flash of binoculars, the blacked-out vans sitting idle by the curb that indicated someone was watching. But the street was still.

A cold wind ruffled her hair. The air was turning cool and damp so fast that the warm air trapped in her car was fogging the windows. Looking to the north, she saw the steel grey clouds of a blue norther.

She let herself in, moving carefully in the dim light that seeped in through half-closed venetian blinds. The living room was furnished for comfort—a large overstuffed couch with matching armchairs, and a coffee table piled high with textbooks, spiral notebooks, and assorted compact discs. The floor was carpeted with a pale Berber rug that was thick enough to feel comfortable without advertising its price.

A breakfast bar separated the living room from the kitchen and a phone sat on the counter. Kate picked up the receiver softly and listened to the dial tone. She thought about checking it for a mike, but if she were going to be really careful, she'd have to check the whole place—light fixtures, phone jacks, on and on. But she really wasn't going to be around long enough for it to matter.

She moved to the bedroom and stopped there, staring at a platform bed as if she could read Lissa's recent history in it. What she saw was a soft blue quilt and two heavy pillows that were propped against the wall to make a backrest. For one person, Kate noted, surprised at how relieved she felt. There were two nightstands, one with a telephone, the other crowded with the kind of paperbacks you saw in college bookstores. A small TV rested on a portable stand at the foot of the bed. Something to watch when you had trouble falling asleep. Kate imagined Lissa here, sitting up against the pillows, reading and flipping from channel to channel.

She opened the closet and leaned in for a look. She found the usual jeans, some shirts, two running suits and, closest to her, a dress smelling of bitter lemon. No sign of Jimmy's clothes.

The last room was the bathroom. Kate checked the shower and, for no good reason, the medicine cabinet. She told herself she was just being careful, but knew she was really looking for signs of Jimmy. She found a single toothbrush, some makeup and a tiny pink razor.

She went back to the kitchen and pulled herself up on a stool next to the phone. She should try Gruber again. Sure, he'd have a fit, but the plain fact was that they had failed. Bud Porter wasn't around Corpus and it didn't really matter anyway. Wherever he was, he was an old man. Sooner or later he'd die. As for her, she'd caused all the deaths she ever wanted to. If Gruber wanted to be famous, he could do it without her help.

She thought about leaving a note instead of waiting. There was a spiral notebook in the bedroom. She ripped out three sheets of paper, returned to the living room, turned on the stereo, and sorted through the compact discs looking for something that would suit the occasion—music for shitheads, maybe. She settled for Stevie Ray Vaughn's last album and eased herself onto the couch. Then she looked at the blank paper. All she had to do was start writing, but nothing came. She leaned back and closed her eyes. In another minute she'd sit up and get the damned thing written. She'd take a second, just to rest her eyes.

The next sound she heard was the door opening. She sat up with a start, but it was Lissa pushed in by a rush of cold air. She was carrying a grocery bag, which she placed on the kitchen counter. "You have any trouble getting in?" she said.

Kate pulled herself up. "Key was right where you said it'd be." The sheets of paper fluttered to the floor.

Lissa took a six-pack of Pearl beer out of the bag and popped two cans out of their plastic rings. She brought one to Kate. She poured her own in a glass. "You hear about the shooting in town?" she said.

"I was there."

"Figures." She took a drink. "So what happened?"

"Somebody was after me."

Lissa moved close to her and put an arm around her shoulder. "Baby, what are you into?" she asked. Her voice was soft and intense, and she searched Kate's face as if the answer might show up there. "You have to tell me."

Kate took a deep breath. And then she told her.

Lissa sat across from her, her mouth growing tighter and her jaw twitching slightly. She got those white little lines around her eyes that meant she was about to lose it. Kate forced herself to keep on talking.

"Is that all?" Lissa's voice was artificially calm.

Kate nodded carefully. She was perched on the edge of the couch, waiting. When they were in Lexington she'd seen Lissa break a chapel bench over a woman's head because she'd called her a piece of tornado bait.

Lissa must have been gripping her glass too tightly, because it shattered, spilling first beer, then blood from cuts on her hand, onto the carpet. She clutched her hand to her chest and headed to the kitchen. Books and papers scattered everywhere. Kate stood up to go to her.

"Don't you touch me." Lissa was at the sink rinsing her injured hand. Blood-red water ran down the drain. She spoke to Kate without looking up. "You've destroyed me. Do you know that? You've ruined my life."

Kate looked at a drawn venetian blind. There was nothing to say. Lissa was right.

"Don't you stand there looking like a martyr." Lissa was facing her now. "You come in here and wreck everything chasing some old man who isn't even here!" Her voice got higher and louder.

Kate raised her hands. "I never expected—"

Lissa cut her off. "Oh, I know you never expected. You asshole. You never planned on hurting anybody. All you wanted to do was kill your father. So you go undercover like some slimy little snitch, and get Jimmy and Joe Ray and God only knows who else after you. And you make good and sure to get me right in the middle of it. Do you know what happened to the last person who snitched on them? The only piece of him they ever found was his head floating in Nueces River with the eyelids chewed off."

"Jesus Christ." Kate felt heat rise in her chest. "You got no right yelling at me. You're living like a queen and telling yourself everything is just great, but you know what these scumbag friends of yours do? They sell drugs to black people and guns to white people who want to shoot them. You shared fucking cells with women who were inside because of people like Jimmy. These are the worst people in the country, you asshole, and you're right in there with them."

Lissa gave her a hard look. Her eyes had the teary, red look that Kate knew to be anger. She made herself take a deep breath and lower her voice.

"I've got some cash," Kate said. "You can take what I have and get out of here." It was lame, but it was all she had to offer. "I'll take enough for bus fare. You can take the rest and get out of here."

Lissa took a paper towel and wrapped it around her hand. "I don't

165

need your money." She looked into the distance for a moment, then went to the phone. She dialed a number and waited. "Rick," her voice was cold, all business, "I need you to take me to New Orleans right away." She listened intently. "I don't give a shit about cold fronts. I need to go tonight." Then she stopped again, listening. "Okay, call me first thing."

"Can you get out?" Kate said.

Lissa shook her head. "He says we're socked in. Heavy fog and ice. Nothing's moving down here tonight. He'll call as soon as it's clear."

With Kate following, she walked to the door and opened it to test the air. The temperature had dropped some thirty degrees since the wind shifted. A fog with freezing rain had blown in, obscuring the view of the houses on the opposite side of the street. Kate took a tentative step onto the sidewalk. It was covered with a thin sheet of ice. Port Aransas was on an island. Once the bridges and roads froze over, it might as well be on another planet, because nobody would be going anywhere till the salt trucks came through.

Lissa was bleeding through the paper towel. Kate led her to the bathroom and seated her on the toilet seat while she rummaged through the medicine cabinet for gauze and iodine.

She knelt beside Lissa and bent over her hand. "This is going to hurt."

Lissa looked away.

Kate daubed the cuts gently, then leaned over to blow on them they way her grandmother had blown on bruises and cuts to make the pain go away.

Lissa's face softened and her eyes seemed to grow wider. She had the look of a little girl at the doctor's office. Kate carefully bandaged her palm, then held her hand a moment longer. She took a tissue and wiped Lissa's eyes. Then she leaned forward and started to kiss her. Lissa pulled away a moment, then allowed Kate to pull her close.

At first they kissed tentatively, like they might hurt each other. Kate took Lissa's face in her hands and kissed her easily, gently, first one kiss and then another. Lissa put her arms around Kate, hugging her, and Kate bent to kiss Lissa's neck. There was this one little

166

place—so soft and sweet, just like she remembered.

Around midnight, they found their way out from under the covers. Lissa'd brought two orders of ribs from Corpus. They ate picnic-style in the middle of the bed. Later, after they'd shoved the debris aside and made love again, Lissa drew them a bath. She got into the tub first and opened her arms for Kate to slide in.

Kate lay in the warm soapy water. Something kept nagging at her. "Are you sure you're going to be able to get out of here?"

"Baby, all I need is to get to that plane. I mean, you don't hang out with Jimmy very long before you figure out he's not long-term relationship material. Hell, he has a wife and kids up in Beeville."

"So what's your plan?"

"I've got an offshore account and a clean passport. I'll go someplace where the dollar's strong. You need to worry about what you're going to do."

Kate shrugged. Life underground was nothing new to her. "I just want to be sure you're prepared."

"Katie, I started preparing the first time Jimmy took me to Brother Dwight Porter's winter conference."

Despite the warm water, Kate felt a chill. She pulled herself up and turned around to face Lissa. "What is this conference?"

"Brother Dwight has a meeting down in Aruba every year or so. It's for managers and moneymen. No press, no candidates. Girlfriends, but no wives."

"What's the agenda?"

Lissa smiled. "He lays out the elections, the candidates and the costs. Especially the costs. He lets them know what their assessment will be."

Kate tried to take this in. She pushed a drop of water out of her eyes. "You're saying Dwight is running Jimmy and Joe Ray?"

"More than those two. He has all kinds of people, even some from Mexico."

Kate was still confused. "So what are they're doing"

Lissa spoke slowly, like she was explaining the theory of relativity to a three-year-old. "Dwight has this plan to put a man in the White

House. He figures if he can elect enough congressmen and senators, he'll end up in control of the Republican Party. When he gets a man in the White House, he'll be the kingmaker."

"So where do Jimmy and Joe Ray come in?"

"Elections cost money. Dwight says they're using dirty money to make a clean country. And, honey, when televangelists start talking about running the country, I just know it's time to get my bags packed and ready."

Kate was stunned. She knew Dwight was interested in politics, but nothing like this. "What are all these guys going to get out of helping Dwight?"

"Access, control. Jimmy says with friends in Washington, the whole business climate will change. He and Joe Ray might even go legit."

"And all the Christian stuff?"

Lissa tossed her head impatiently, "That kind of thing didn't mean shit to anybody down there."

Kate leaned so far back she fell into the faucet. She felt like her chest had sprung a leak, and she was growing smaller by the second. If she wasn't careful, she'd slide down the drain with the bath water. So there it was. She'd been chasing her tail. Both she and her father were irrelevant. There was a whole show going on right in front of her, and she hadn't even seen it.

She reached to touch Lissa's hair, like it was some kind of talisman, and Lissa took her hand and kissed it. "You feeling okay?" she asked.

Kate only nodded because she was afraid she'd start crying if she tried to speak.

"You don't look so good," Lissa said. She got out of the tub and pulled Kate along, wrapping Kate in her robe while she toweled her hair dry.

Later they made love again and curled under the down quilt in Lissa's bed. Afterward, Kate rested on her back with Lissa's head on her shoulder. In the background, Joe Henderson played sax on an Ellington tune called "Chelsea Bridge." Kate beat the time with her right finger, gently, so as not to disturb Lissa. This night would only come once, and she didn't want to waste it sleeping.

But she woke to grey light filtering though the blinds. For awhile, she rested in the soft smells of love and sleep, but eventually an ache in her left arm forced her to shift, and she rose slowly, without waking Lissa.

She gathered her clothes and tiptoed to the kitchen, where she searched until she found a coffee canister. The fridge was nearly empty. No eggs, no milk. She dressed and left the house, taking care to lock the door behind her.

She'd meant to drive to the Maverick convenience store on the blacktop highway, but her windows were covered with glazed ice. She pried open the car door with her fingers and searched inside for a scraper, but this was Texas and rental cars didn't carry ice scrapers.

She set off on foot, walking beside the curbs, and crossed a sandy field and an icy, deserted parking lot. The wind gusted out of the north, cutting through the canvas jacket she'd taken from a hook inside the front door. She stuffed her fists into her pockets to warm her hands, but by the time she reached the store her nose and ears were stinging with cold.

Inside, the clerk stood transfixed in front of a television, where a woman wearing a red blazer and an inane smile pointed at a weather map of the state of Texas and recited temperatures. There were blizzard conditions in the Panhandle, freezing rain in Dallas and San Antonio. No travel was advised in central Texas. Corpus, she said, would not see snow but there would be continued freezing rain and hazardous driving. Drivers could expect to find roads and bridges closed.

"Looks like a real norther," the clerk said, happy to have something to talk about.

Kate bought a carton of eggs, some flour, juice, milk and a bottle of syrup. Just before she reached the counter she turned back and took a package of sausage. It would go good with pancakes.

A driving rain followed her back to the house. The streets had become slicker and she almost fell on the front step.

The front door was unlocked, the kitchen lights were on, and the house smelled of coffee. She felt a sudden stir behind her and started to turn, but someone grabbed her neck and pulled her close. It was an old man's arm that held her, but it was a strong one. She dropped the grocery bag and flailed, trying to get enough traction to aim a backward strike with her right foot—with luck she could take out a knee— but she felt a cold muzzle jam into her cheek.

"Slow down, Sister." The voice behind her was a familiar one. "It's just your daddy."

CHAPTER TWENTY-NINE

Her father's arm tightened around her neck, threatening to cut off her air. Across the room, Lissa, still wearing her bathrobe, stood frozen by the stove. Both hands were at her mouth, stifling a scream.

"Get her out of here," Kate said, struggling against her father's arm. "She doesn't need to be involved in this."

Her father slackened his hold just enough to let her breathe a little easier, but the muzzle remained in place. "She can go or stay," he said. He lowered the weapon and released her.

"Go," she said to Lissa.

Lissa shook her head.

Kate turned slightly to her father. "Tell her to go."

"I didn't come here to kill you, Sister." Her father moved around to face her. He spoke in the kind of reasonable voice you might use to persuade someone to lower their weapon. "If that's what I wanted you'd be dead already. I just want to have a talk with you."

Kate took a good look at him. Age had made him lean and sharp, eliminating the layer of fat she remembered from his Kansas days. And he must have gotten some new teeth, because his jawline was no longer slack. His military buzz cut was grizzled, but the eyes still had their butane-blue sharpness. They could drill a hole in steel plate.

He gave her a fatherly smile that made her feel like a toddler with a skinned knee, but his weapon remained cocked. He used it to gesture toward a stool at the counter.

She moved cautiously, with the feeling that she should lace her hands behind her head the way they did in jail when there was a weapons search. She slid herself onto the stool, and Bud took the one beside her. He glanced in Lissa's direction.

"Why don't you bring us some of that coffee?" he said. When she did, he rested his weapon on the counter and took a long sip from his cup. Then he turned again to face Kate. "You know you did wrong back there at Hutch, don't you, Sister? A lot of good men went down on account of you."

"Yes, sir." She could have kicked her own butt for letting him make her act like she was ten years old.

"By rights I ought to kill you for that."

"But it was okay for you to drive off and leave us there?" She started to lift her cup, but her hand shook so badly the coffee spilled. Bud reached for a napkin and handed it to her.

"It wouldn't have changed a thing if I'd stayed there. You know that." He looked at her for a long moment until she dropped her eyes. "But you did your time," he said. "Stand-up time, too." He took another sip of coffee. "Dwight told me he tried to get you to take the easy way, but you wouldn't do it."

"You still see Dwight?" Her voice was shaky.

Her father gave a snort of a laugh. "Oh yes. At least when he isn't hiding out in Virginia."

"So what's this about?" She stopped herself just short of calling him Daddy.

"I might as well ask you that, Sister. You come here with that guy from Kansas and start hanging with that dirty cop, Charlie Watson."

Kate worked to keep her face bland. He must have had her under surveillance from the minute she arrived. He'd been sitting back, watching her every move.

Her father gave her a slow smile. "I guess I can understand you'd be a little upset. Hell, I might have done the same thing myself if it'd been me inside. So, I just let you poke around until you figured out what was going on and cooled down a little."

The thought of him watching while she stumbled around town playing detective was too much. Her voice came back and the words tumbled out before she could stop them. "Oh, I think I got that figured, all right. You turned the APF into a bunch of gunrunners. You got them hauling drugs in from Mexico and trading them for guns up here

172

and then selling them all over the country."

"See?" he turned to Lissa in an appeal. "That's what I mean. She thinks she knows it all, but she doesn't understand shit about what's really happening."

Kate looked at Lissa and shook her head slightly, warning her to stay out of this.

Bud moved his stool closer. "That goddamned brother of yours started that mess. That son of a bitch waited till I went underground and stole my whole damned organization right out from under me. First he starts telling me we need to make some changes. Said we were out of step with the times. Told me the drugs were going to be an income source. We bring in drugs and split the profits with him. We could use the money to buy arms for our people, and he could finance all this election stuff he's got going on. He said he could buy me some protection, even a pardon one of these days." Bud shook his head as if surprised at his own stupidity. "So my boys are strutting around like a bunch of Columbian drug lords, packing Uzis and driving Grand Cherokees. He's taking the money and buying television commercials for those pretty boys he's running for office. You see the posters for that Anderson?" His eyes flared with righteous indignation. "My money's paying for that trash."

Kate glanced uneasily at Lissa. Bud didn't look like he cared at all about her listening to him. That wasn't like him—unless he meant to kill them both.

"I finally called him on it. Told him to meet me up in Branson, Missouri. Said I wasn't going to stand for this. You know what he did?" It wasn't really a question and Bud gave her no time to answer. "He tried setting me up. Had the local heat set a trap for me. Damn near got me, too."

He'd worked himself up to a full speech, and Kate had the feeling this wasn't the first time he'd made it. Then he took a deep breath and slowed himself down. He looked Kate directly in the eye. "So that's what I need you for, Sister."

"You need me?" She couldn't keep the disbelief out of her voice.

"You and me got to take hold of this thing and take that son of a bitch out. He's too insulated for me to get to him. But you could. You two were always close and he'd trust you. I know he would."

"And you want me to help you..." Kate paused, at a loss for words, "...kill Dwight?"

"That's right. For the good of the movement." He nodded his head for emphasis.

Kate looked down at her coffee cup, trying to think of a way to be diplomatic, but nothing came to mind. So she decided to just say it. "You think you can come here, and I'll jump right on board and go kill my brother." She'd never taken that kind of voice with him, and her tone was strong enough to make her father blink.

"Sister, I'm not telling you stories. I think you deserve a real chance and I'm willing to give it to you." He clapped an arm around her to pull her close. Kate resisted the pull of his arm.

"What if I don't want to?"

"God, I'd be sorry to hear that." Bud's arm dropped and his face clouded. He sounded genuinely stricken. "There'd be no way back, then. If you're not with me, you're against me."

"What if I just want to be out of the whole thing?"

"I know you think that's what you want, but that's because you haven't accepted your part in things. You're my daughter. You can't ever be out of the plan."

"And what if I don't believe a word you're saying?" Kate's voice had grown harder.

"Shit, Sister, you know the answer to that."

Kate looked at him for a long, blazing minute. Lissa stood at the periphery of her vision, reaching for the coffee pot. Kate gave a tiny nod. Bud was reaching for his weapon, but she launched herself at him before he could raise it. Lissa got him in the head with the coffeepot. Their combined force knocked him off the stool and onto his back. Kate grabbed the weapon, a Browning Hi-Power. She leveled it at him. Bud lay on the floor, groaning in pain that would have made anyone else scream at the top of their lungs. Half of his face was bright red and one eye was burned shut. He covered it with his hand and looked up at her with one blue eye. "You're going to have to shoot me, Sister. Think you can do that?" Pain made him gasp for breath.

Kate didn't answer. She kept the Browning pointed at him and fought to keep her hand from shaking.

"You can't," Bud said. "You don't have it in you."

The Browning began to shake slightly. She gripped her right hand with her left, but the shaking only got worse.

Bud pulled himself partway up and reached toward his boot top. He'd have another weapon there, probably a .38, strapped to his calf. He pulled his pant leg up slightly. "You know you can't do it."

Kate fired and the bullet propelled him back to the floor, but not before his skull shattered, shooting his brain toward the wall behind him. He convulsed four or five times before his nervous system ground to a stop. Then he gave one last shudder and his body released its contents.

Kate and Lissa stood there, watching it happen. Then Kate knelt and put her hand on his chest. The last blood was still pumping, but already he felt lifeless. It was over. She sat back on her heels and looked down at the Browning as if it had done the firing all by itself. She rose and carried it delicately to the counter. Then she took a napkin and wiped it clean of fingerprints.

"You need to get out of here," she said to Lissa.

"You're going to need a witness."

"No, you got to go."

Kate stood by her father's body while Lissa got dressed. The smell of coffee mixed with the smell of death. A split bag of groceries lay scattered onto the carpet, and, at her feet, her father's blood seeped onto the floor. The wall behind was covered with blood and fragments of tissue. Fallen against it, her father's body had the same rag-doll look Viola McKinnon's body had that terrible day back in Hutchinson.

When Lissa came out of the bedroom, she'd put on jeans and a workshirt. She moved close and touched Kate's cheek gently, but Kate stepped back.

"You don't have to stay here," Lissa said. "Take my car. I'll take yours. We can meet up in Houston."

Kate looked off into the distance. She couldn't bring herself to meet Lissa's eye. "Just go," she said.

"I'm not going anywhere without you."

"Okay." Kate had to think fast. "I'll meet you tomorrow at—" she stopped for a minute to think of a hotel chain "—the downtown Marriott in Houston."

She had to get things moving quickly, before her voice broke and she lost all of her resolve. She pulled Lissa to her and held her very close, allowing herself to feel her hair and that very soft space where her neck and shoulder met.

And then she was gone and Kate was alone with her father's body. She knelt beside him and brushed the undamaged part of his face softly with her hand. It was a gesture from her childhood, when she used to sneak up to the couch where her father napped and brush his hair gently to make him smile.

To her surprise, her eyes filled with tears. Back in Lexington, when she'd imagined killing him, it had always been easy. She'd thought his death would bring a sense of release, that justice had been done, that scores would have been settled. But kneeling beside him here now, all she felt was sorrow. She bent and kissed her father's dead cheek.

"I'm sorry, Daddy," she said softly, "I really am."

CHAPTER THIRTY

The fog lifted enough to let her see Lissa's car fishtail as it turned the corner at the end of the block and then vanish. She looked around, searching for Bud's vehicle, but there was no telling how he'd gotten out there. He could have talked his way on board a sanding truck or hitched a ride with an emergency vehicle.

She found a blanket in the bedroom and draped it over her father's body. Then she knelt beside the covered corpse. This would be the time to say a prayer, but she didn't know who she'd be praying for. She stood up and went back to the bedroom to make a call.

When Gruber answered, she said, "Its me. I think I'm in some trouble."

He listened to her story. "Have you called the locals yet?"

"No."

"Okay, just sit tight. I'll be there as soon as I can."

The living room was out so she tried the bedroom, but it still smelled of Lissa. That drove her out the kitchen door, and she circled around to wait in her car, slumped with exhaustion, making no effort to get her story straight. Something inside had switched off, maybe the part that ran the emotions, because she felt just like a blank, flat piece of slate. Nothing at all. She pushed the seat back till it almost reclined, and she closed her eyes.

The next sound she heard was a car door slamming. Gruber, and Charlie Watson were walking toward the house. She got out and called to them.

"Anyone else here?" Gruber asked.

Kate shook her head.

177

"Whose house is this?"

"It belongs to Sally Rushing, but she wasn't here." Kate tried to slow her words down. Talking too fast usually meant you were lying. Gruber's eyes narrowed a little, but he didn't ask how it was she happened to be there.

"Let's have a look." Charlie opened the door and he and Gruber stepped inside. Kate forced herself onto the porch. The wind drove icy rain through her jacket. She felt her nose begin to run with the chill, and she jammed her hands into her pockets, but didn't go in.

When the two men emerged, they wore the stoic looks policemen put on around the recently dead, like if they let themselves feel anything they'd fall apart completely.

"Let's go," Gruber said.

They'd come out in an unmarked Sheriff's Department car. Kate wanted to drive her own car back to town, but Gruber shook his head when she suggested it. He motioned for her to get into the back seat. Something in his manner told her not to argue, so she got in the back, which was separated from the front by a mesh grill. The plastic upholstery was sticky with something she didn't want to know about, and when the door shut, it locked her inside.

"Where are we going?" she said.

Gruber ignored her question. Instead, he peppered her with questions. Kate kept her answers short, just skirting the edges of the truth. She was betting they hadn't checked the body closely enough to see the burn marks on Bud's face. Neither man challenged her.

Charlie drove cautiously. Still, when he came to the first stop sign, he slid right through the intersection before coming to a stop and killing the engine. After that he drove at a crawl. Every time he tried to speed up, the car slipped to the side of the road. Gruber was silent. He sat staring straight ahead like he thought he could hold the car on the road by force of will.

Kate was grateful for the chance to think about why she'd been at Lissa McEvoy's house. She could have gone there to wait for Lissa and have it out with her about all the stuff that went on at Lexington. Or maybe she knew about the place and had broken into it to hide after someone took a shot at her. Gruber might get mad at her for not letting him know, but, hell, she'd called, even if it wasn't for that reason. She hadn't been able to reach him.

It must have taken forty-five minutes to reach the highway into Corpus, which should have been a fifteen minute drive. The fog reduced the traffic signal to a distant glow. A right turn would take them back toward town, but Charlie swung left and crept forward while Gruber leaned toward the dashboard looking intently into the fog.

"Where we going?" Kate asked.

"Just sit tight," Charlie said.

That was when she started to get scared.

CHAPTER THIRTY-ONE

Gruber and Charlie kept their eyes on the road as if there were no one at all in the back seat. Kate waited till she could be sure her voice wouldn't shake. "Where we going? Ray?"

Charlie answered. "We're making a stop."

"What kind of stop?" But she knew. When the car took the road away from Corpus, she knew she was on a one-way trip. All of sudden she was so mad that hot tears, the kind she really hated, came to her eyes, and she had to sniff hard to keep her nose from running.

"Now don't start bawling." Charlie turned his head slightly. "We're just trying to save your life."

"Sure you are." Kate leaned hard against the seat behind her. She clenched and unclenched her fists and promised herself she wouldn't go without a fight. If she was fast enough, she could level a kick to Charlie's knees. He might shield his groin, but he couldn't cover everything. Gruber would grab her, but she should be able to get in a punch or two before he dropped her.

A momentary gap in the fog gave her a glimpse of houses on large lots with winding canals and docks in the rear. It looked like the same neighborhood where she'd gone to the party, but before she could get a closer look, the fog closed in again. A few minutes later, they pulled to a stop in front of a brick house with a huge oak door.

Gruber got out first and let Kate out before Charlie had time to extract himself. Gruber was too close for a kick so she aimed at Charlie as he rounded the car, but she was too slow. Gruber grabbed her from behind.

"For Christ's sake, Kate, settle down," he said.

She used her left elbow to send a sharp blow to his abdomen. Gruber tightened his hold.

"Want me to cuff her?" Charlie was reaching behind his back for his handcuffs.

"If you're going to do me, just do it right here," Kate yelled as loud as she could.

"Somebody wants to talk to you. That's all." Gruber spoke into her ear. "You going to settle down?"

Kate tried to raise a knee so she could slam her foot back into Gruber's knee, but he felt it coming. He kicked her support leg out from under her, causing her to fall.

He caught her in his arms. "I mean it. Nobody's going to hurt you."

Kate nodded grudgingly. They had her for now. She'd have to wait for another chance.

Charlie Watson shook his head in disgust. "I oughta cuff her."

Gruber loosened his hold now and stood beside Kate. "She'll be okay." He turned to Kate. "Won't you?"

She nodded again.

They entered through a side gate that opened onto a pool and a white stucco poolhouse. Charlie and Gruber guided her toward the poolhouse. An automatic door swung open, and Charlie pushed her into a stark white room, furnished only with computer tables, printer stands and file cabinets. The light was so bright it made her squint. It took her a minute before she could make out a dark figure at the far end of the room. It was Dwight, seated in his wheelchair.

She was struck by how different he looked from his television image. The camera managed to reduce the contrast between his tiny, useless legs and his huge torso, but it was more than that: his face had thickened with age. Dwight used to worry that he had a baby face. When they were in high school, he kept his eyebrows knitted so he'd look tougher. Now he had succeeded. He had the eyes of a man who'd seen everything a human being is capable of doing.

"Sister." It was the first time he'd ever called her that name. "'Bout time we got together."

Kate closed her eyes, in pain at her own stupidity as much as anything else. It had been here all along, right in front of her.

"I've been a little busy." She tried to keep her voice light.

Gruber and Charlie stood on either side of her, just two cops guarding a prisoner.

"You get him?" Dwight addressed the question to the two men.

"He's dead," Gruber answered.

"You checked," Dwight asked.

"Checked him myself," Charlie said.

"He's dead, Dwight," Kate said. "I shot him. He's all the way dead."

Dwight gave a sharp nod—a piece of ugly business finished.

"I'm sorry it fell to you to do that. I really meant for someone else to take care of that part. But, damn," he turned to Gruber, "didn't I tell you he'd come out once he knew she was here?" Gruber started to answer, but Dwight cut him off. "Charlie, get her a chair. You boys wait outside for me."

Charlie looked surprised, like he wasn't used to taking orders, but he rolled an armless steno chair over for Kate and he and Gruber left.

"So this was it, Dwight? This whole thing was to get Daddy?" Kate was surprised at how sad she sounded.

"Sister, I'm sorry to get you involved in this, but I figured you'd be coming after him on your own." Dwight's voice was full of concern and reason.

"So you just set me up to kill him." Kate's voice broke. "Damn it, Dwight, I thought we were family." She wanted ask him how he could do this to her after all they'd been through together, but she didn't want to break down in front of him.

"Sister, you had to know this was coming. You saw what he was like. We talked about it way back there in Wichita." Dwight's voice was impatient, as if he were stating the obvious. "Somebody had to take him out. He was getting ready to rob banks again, and he was going around offering a bounty to the first man who took me out. If we'd let him keep on, he'd have come across some Jew reporter looking for a story and the whole thing would have blown up in our faces."

"If you wanted to catch him, why not do it yourself?"

"Don't think I didn't try. I almost got him once or twice, but he was too good. He had himself a couple of snipers that would never have left me alone. You remember that Lloyd Hughes up in Amarillo?" Dwight made a gesture to the north. "He was one of them. He says he works for me, but that backshooting piece of slime would turn on me in a heartbeat. He'd end up costing me a fortune in bodyguards. Him and that Weldon Sanford from Dumas would have been waiting round every corner for me. What's more, they'd have run out and told everybody what happened and end up busting the APF to smithereens. I couldn't let that happen, Katie. We need it."

"The APF's your own private oil well, right? Just pumping money in."

Dwight nodded with pride. "We're running candidates in seven states. Four of them have a good chance of winning. Elections aren't cheap. We're spending fifty million on TV ads alone."

"Your candidates know about any of this?"

Dwight gave her a broad smile. "My candidates are not chosen for their inquiring minds. Mr. Anderson is upstairs right now, resting up from porking a cheerleader from Southern Methodist University. He'll be down after while. He's looking forward to meeting you."

Sure he is, Kate thought. "And Gruber? Where'd he come into it?"

"Raymond and I started talking back there at your trial. He's kept in touch."

"But you just had to get me to do it."

Dwight shrugged. "You wanted a chance to even the score. You know you did. So I gave it to you." He paused for a moment, frowning. "But don't think I'm going to let you take the rap for this." He shook his head, all sincere generosity. "Not for a second."

He moved his wheelchair slightly. "We'll get you out of the country. You can go anywhere you want. You got the money Grandma left you. We'll get you a clean passport and set you up." He gave her an encouraging smile. "You've earned it."

It sounded so nice that it wasn't hard for her to smile back. But there was no way Dwight could let her go off on her own. She knew too much. He certainly couldn't afford to let her get arrested. The local heat might not believe her story, but the right reporter would.

From where she stood, it looked like the only place she was going was the bottom of the bay, or some shallow grave out where nobody'd ever find her.

Dwight clapped his hands together. "I don't know about you, Sister, but I'm hungry. Let's round up those boys and go have some breakfast."

He wheeled himself toward the door, which swung open as he approached. Gruber and Charlie were lounging outside, Charlie smoking a cigarette and Gruber looking morose.

Dwight wheeled past and motioned for them to follow. "I feel like having me a plate of eggs and grits." He sounded expansive.

The mention of food made Kate feel queasy. She wasn't sure she'd ever want to eat again, even if she lived long enough to get the chance.

The buzz of a cell phone interrupted her thoughts. Gruber reached inside his jacket to check his, but shook his head. Dwight halted his chair and frowned like he was trying to remember what made that sound, then reached inside his suit jacket. He wheeled the chair ahead a few feet to give himself the illusion of privacy, then held the receiver to his ear and said, "Yeah." It wasn't the preacherly answer Kate had expected. This must be his private, private line.

Dwight's face was impassive as he listened. Whoever he was talking to had a lot to say.

The call ended when Dwight gave a heavy sigh and said, "I'll call you back in ten minutes." He lowered the phone, pushed the disconnect button, and rested it in his lap for a minute before slipping it into his jacket as if it were a fragile piece of crystal.

"Raymond," he said. His voice was flat and dead.

Gruber moved to his side.

"Something's come up. Take my sister back to the office and keep her company."

Gruber turned toward Kate.

"What—" Charlie started to say.

"Just do it." Dwight wheeled toward him. His voice was like stone falling on stone.

They walked back to the office. Kate took the chair, Gruber leaned against the wall by the door, and Charlie propped himself up on a long white worktable. A phone rang twice activating a fax machine, which began to cough out paper. Charlie gave a couple of dry hacks, then blew his nose into a tiny wad of Kleenex he drew from his jacket.

"When was it you got to know him, Ray?" Kate asked.

Gruber sighed heavily. "I met him back when you were in the Sedgewick County jail."

"And when did you start working for him?"

Charlie snorted. "You don't have to tell her anything."

"No, its okay." Gruber said. "It was kind of gradual. He was interested in catching your father. He asked if we could share information."

"And he put you on the payroll," Kate prompted him.

"Yeah." Gruber looked off in the distance. "It was my ex."

"The bitch." Charlie said.

"She cleaned out the savings accounts before she left. Judge hit me with nine hundred and sixty dollars a month child support for kids I don't even see. Hell, she even got into my pension fund."

Kate nodded. When people sell you out, they always have a good reason for it. "So why'd you let me fool around following Jimmy Tyler?"

It was Charlie who answered. "'Cause I was in Houston for a couple of days, that's why. He was supposed to check in with me every day, but Ace here thought he might have run onto another hot collar." Charlie glared at Gruber, who didn't meet his eye and looked at the floor as if he wanted to find something there. The only sounds were vines brushing against the window, and Charlie's occasional dry, cigarette cough.

Some twenty minutes later, the door swung open, and Dwight wheeled in, followed by a flat-faced man built like a professional wrestler. His black turtleneck and leather jacket heightened the effect.

"Raymond, Charlie, could you excuse us." It wasn't a request, but the two men hesitated. "Go on," Dwight said, "you don't want to hear what we're going to talk about."

Gruber looked at Charlie, who gave him the kind of shrug that says, who knows? They left.

Dwight wheeled impatiently past Kate. The other man arranged himself by the doorway and folded his arms across his chest. Kate could have been just another piece of equipment. She was tired of waiting and tired of listening. Most of all, she was tired of her brother. "What happens now, Dwight? You going to have me shot while trying to escape?"

Dwight wheeled to face her. His jaw twitched slightly. "I just got a phone call from Jimmy Tyler's whore of a girlfriend. Sally, isn't that her name?" He turned slightly toward the guard who nodded in confirmation. "She says you told her you might be here, says she knew you in prison." His voice sounded tired and hoarse. "She's saying Jimmy tried to have you shot. That true?"

Kate nodded.

"How come was that?"

Kate gave him a look of disgust. "How the hell would I know? Maybe he thought I was setting him up for a gun-running bust. Maybe he thought I was after his woman." She paused for effect. "Maybe he just needed the practice."

Dwight wheeled back and forth like a man pacing in anger. "Slimy little bottom feeder. His woman is fixing to blackmail me, and he's out trying to have you killed."

Kate repressed a smile. Lissa must have been paying close attention during those conferences on Aruba. "What difference does it make who does me?"

"You're my sister, that's what difference it makes." Dwight wheeled to face her.

"And if anyone kills me, it'll be you," Kate said.

From the doorway the guard gave a little cough like he was signaling it was time to get moving.

"So this red-headed piece of trash calls me up and tells me that she's got transcripts stored in some bank somewhere and copies with her lawyer in Sinton. And if she doesn't hear from you in one hour she'll have him go public with the whole thing." Dwight's voice rose in anger. "Shit, I could kill the stories, but she's talking federal attorney." He nodded to himself as if he were watching his enemies savor their triumph.

"She left a number for you to call at," Dwight glanced at his watch, "Eleven A.M. sharp and once an hour till this afternoon. Then you're supposed to get over to Sinton to see this lawyer. Some guy named Ben Stone."

"And if I don't show up?"

"If Mr. Stone fails to certify that you are alive and well, she's gonna talk to everybody from the U.S. Attorney to the *New York* fucking *Times*." His voice was flat and resigned.

Kate nodded in agreement. She kept her face as blank as possible. It was never good to push a cornered man—and Dwight was cornered.

Dwight wheeled himself over to a desk and began examining some papers there. After an awkward minute or two, the guard turned to leave.

"Earl, I want you to go find Jimmy right away." Dwight took a pen off the desk and raised it to his mouth like it was a cigarette. "And when you find him, take his weapon and blow off the back of his fucking head."

"Seriously?"

Dwight gave him a look that would wither a rosebush.

The guard nodded curtly and left.

Dwight slumped slightly in his chair and fell into a long silence. Kate stood up to leave, but he motioned for her to stay.

"You ever wonder what it would have been like if Mama had lived?" His voice was soft and reflective. "You ever think about that?"

"I used to."

Dwight studied her as if he were seeing her for the first time. "If you'd let your hair grow and put on a little makeup, you'd look a lot like her."

Kate smiled sadly. She had no way of knowing whether Dwight was right because Daddy had destroyed all the pictures of their mother.

Dwight nodded to himself, as if he'd reached a conclusion, and cleared his throat. "Here's the plan," he said. "You've got till Daddy's body's found. That ought to be enough time to get out of here." He paused, looking at her with the cold, clear gaze she'd only seen before in her father's eyes. "You don't make that call, we give you up for murdering your daddy. Clear?"

"Clear."

"Then get your perverted ass out of here." He spun his chair in place and rolled through the doorway at the far end of the room, leaving the door swinging back and forth in the silence.

Outside, the wind was dying but fog still hung over the island. A man who looked like one of the security guards from the candidate's fund-raising party drove her to town. Driving was easier now. The roads must have been salted because the car held to the pavement. The driver was silent until they reached the outskirts of Corpus.

"Any place special you want to be dropped?" he asked.

"Right here'll be fine."

The car slowed and Kate opened the door to leave. The guard smiled slightly.

"You take care, hear. We'll be looking for you."

"Yeah," Kate said. She'd be looking for them too.

She walked to a Maverick store, where she used the outside pay phone to call Lissa's number. She got a recording of Lissa's anxious voice speaking over what sounded like airport noise.

"Katie, the man you need to see is Ben Stone in Sinton. He's waiting for you at his office. Go there right away." There was a pause. Kate heard the sound of flights being called in the background. "And be careful, baby."

The message ended there.

Kate replaced the receiver and leaned back against the wall. The sky around her grew lighter as the fog lifted, allowing her to see the tall slabs of condominiums overlooking the gulf. She was too tired to cry and too empty to feel fear. All she could feel was love.

CHAPTER THIRTY-TWO

The air was a little warmer and traffic was slowly starting to move. Still, Kate had to stand in driving rain for half an hour before a Lone Star beer truck gave her a lift to Port Aransas. The moment she climbed into the warm cab, waves of exhaustion swept over her. She had to strain to listen as the driver told her that his name was Ted and he wasn't supposed to pick up hitchhikers, but in this weather it was the only Christian thing to do.

The truck dropped her off near the pier, and she walked the six blocks to Lissa's house, where she'd left her car. The lights were still on inside. All she'd have to do was push the door open and go in, but nothing on earth would make her go back into that house.

She drove to the ferry that connected Port Aransas to the causeway leading to Aransas Pass. The trip took less than five minutes. Tired-looking pelicans huddled on the jetty like the prisoners in the yard at Lexington on a cold day. Just a bunch of sad, down-and-out birds taking a break from the grinding labor of feeding themselves.

She knew she should go straight to the lawyer's office, but the only thing in the world she wanted was a shower. So she phoned the number and left a message on his machine. Just the other side of Aransas Pass she spotted a ma-and-pa motel. It was the kind of place that was too small and too close to the road to appeal to winter Texans, so there might be a vacancy.

A shrunken old man with sad eyes signed her in and took her cash. He kept his eyes down, like he didn't want to be able to identify her if he were asked to. She took her key, found her room, and threw her bag on the bed. Then she went directly to the shower and let hot water pour over her while she scrubbed her arms and hands, trying to wash off the smells of her brother and of death. Afterward, she wrapped herself in a towel and sat in a chair by the window. The curtain was drawn, but she pushed it aside and watched an aged weather vane tossing back and forth. The sight completely absorbed her, blocking out all other thoughts.

Lawyer Stone's office was on the second floor of an old downtown building. The facade had been modernized, but inside she found a dark, narrow stairway lined with grey linoleum. At the top was an opaque glass door stenciled with the name Benjamin Stone, Esq. It was ajar, so she peeked in and found he had no secretary, just an empty desk with an ancient IBM Selectric in the typewriter well. In the room beyond, Lawyer Stone sat, tipped back in his chair with his elegantly booted feet on the desk. When he saw Kate, he rose to greet her.

Stone was a tall, blond man with long hair pulled back in a ponytail and a gold stud in his right ear. Kate guessed that Lissa had been one of the few clients who paid the full fee because he was the gay lawyer—the one who drew up the wills, pleaded the child custody disputes and handled the insurance appeals for guys who had HIV.

Stone indicated a chair. "My instructions," he said, leaning back comfortably, "are to assure myself that you are in good health." He peered at her. "May I assume that to be the case?"

Stone had the kind of exaggerated Texas accent that seemed to embed a joke in every sentence.

Kate nodded.

"Then I have this packet for you."

Stone swung himself up and walked to an ancient metal safe in a far corner of the room. He squatted in front of it and opened the door to extract a manila envelope. He slid it toward Kate. "This, I believe, is your travel itinerary."

Kate opened the envelope and pulled out its contents. There was a thick stack of one hundred dollar bills and a note in Lissa's sloping hand. She was to go directly to the Sinton airport. A man named Eric Wallace was waiting for her and would fly her to New Orleans. There was more, but she could read it later. Kate folded the note and returned it and the money to the envelope.

"May I ask a favor?" Kate found herself adopting both his accent and his style. Stone waited to hear what it was. "I'd like a pen and paper."

Stone fished a sheet of paper from his center drawer, then extended his own pen, a Mont Blanc. Kate moved her chair closer to the edge of the desk, which was a rich, dark wood, polished to a silky finish. Lawyer Stone had good taste and the money to go with it, apparently. She positioned the paper in front of her as if the angle would make a difference. For a moment she sat, staring at the blank sheet, then she began carefully, printing each word so there would be no doubt about what it said.

"Dwight Porter killed my father, A. Budrow Porter, at Port Aransas, Texas, on November fifteen, at eight thirty-five a.m. I was present as a captive. He was assisted by Lt. Raymond Gruber of the Kansas Bureau of Investigation and Deputy Charles Watson of the Nueces County Sheriff's Department. My father was bound and executed. He was courageous to the end."

Kate signed her name and pushed back from the table.

"Do you have a stamp pad?"

"I do."

Stone fished in his desk until he found it. Kate inked her right thumb on it and then affixed the print beneath her signature.

Without being asked, Stone extended a tissue for the ink and slid an envelope at her. Kate wrote the name Lloyd Hughes and, leaving a large space, she added Amarillo, Texas.

"Would you be kind enough to check the street address?"

Stone nodded.

She looked around until she found a small copier.

Reading her glance, Stone nodded and slid a second envelope her way. Kate addressed this one to Dwight Porter, c/o Anderson Campaign Headquarters.

Knowing Lloyd Hughes was after him might give Dwight a few sleepless nights. Kate smiled to herself. She might not be able to bring the bastard down, but she could sure as hell destroy his peace of mind.

191

Dwight was right about Lloyd Hughes being a backshooter. But Bud had always considered him as loyal as an old yellow dog, and he was one hell of a sniper. He probably wouldn't get close enough to take anybody out, but he sure as hell could make things uncomfortable for the whole bunch of them.

"Would you be kind enough to mail this for me day after tomorrow?"

Stone took the second envelope.

"Your client'll be calling you. When she does, please tell her I'm all right, but I won't be able to meet her. I still have some business to work out with the interested parties." Stone frowned. "And you tell her they want her bad. She should go far and stay down, got that?"

"You sure about that?"

"The people in question have enough on me to keep me quiet. But they can't ever be sure of her. They're counting on me to lead them straight to her."

Stone frowned a moment, then nodded slowly.

Kate stood up to leave and Stone rose to see her out.

Kate paused. "Tell her I love her. And every day that I know she's alive will be a good day for me."

"I will tell her that." Stone spoke carefully, as if repeating a vow.

He walked her downstairs, stopping at the sidewalk.

"If there's anything I can do…" His voice trailed off.

Kate extended her hand. He covered it with both of his. He seemed to want to say more but was unable to find words. They stood on the main street in Sinton, Texas, clasping hands. For all she knew, he was the last person who would ever call her by her given name and she hated to let him go. She squeezed his hand harder and backed away.

It was time to go.